CRUCIBLES OF POWER

THE THREAT OF ANGEALS

BOOK I

C. T. FITZGERALD

BISAC Categories:
FIC009020   FICTION / Fantasy / Epic
FIC009000   FICTION / Fantasy / General

EMERALD
BOOKS

DEDICATION

For our son, Tim, in whom beat the heart of a warrior,

who is now assuredly with the Angeals of Light.

TABLE OF CONTENTS

CHAPTER 1: HELPLESS   1

CHAPTER 2: SUMMONS   10

CHAPTER 3: GO AND LIVE   15

CHAPTER 4: TRANSFORMATION   21

CHAPTER 5: OTHERS   32

CHAPTER 6: CHOICE   38

CHAPTER 7: BOUGHT AND SOLD   44

CHAPTER 8: OVERCOMING FEAR   49

CHAPTER 9: RED LESSON   60

CHAPTER 10: FAMILY   67

CHAPTER 11: SISTERS   78

CHAPTER 12: PATH OF STONE   86

CHAPTER 13: RITUAL   93

CHAPTER 14: THE FIRST CURADH 99

CHAPTER 15: YOU WILL DIE 109

CHAPTER 16: TESTED 116

CHAPTER 17: REJECTION 122

CHAPTER 18: BELL OF NOTICE 130

CHAPTER 19: CHANGE 135

CHAPTER 20: COMMAND 142

CHAPTER 21: MONSTERS 149

CHAPTER 22: REBORN GREEN 160

CHAPTER 23: GAME OF STONES 169

CHAPTER 24: YOU SHALL KILL 180

CHAPTER 25: REVOLT 186

CHAPTER 26: HEROIC FOOLS 195

ABOUT THE AUTHOR 208

chapter 1:

HELPLESS

He would die with his country. He just didn't know when. Kon-r Sighur sat at a square, stone table carved ages ago from mountain rock. His was one of four chairs covered with ancient runes, which encircled a table on a platform chiseled from the island's highest peak, Creogh Radahar. Below, the Muirseol Sea surrounded the Islands of Athlan: the Islands of Joy. Kon-r watched white seagulls wheel above the green ocean far below the ancient seat of power. The stench of sulfur rose to his perch. Much of the main island burned.

He was slightly larger than average with a ruggedly good-looking face, but he wasn't exceptional. His eyes, like the sea below, were a striking blue-green. He wore a simple, white tunic to his knees with sleeves that covered his elbows. Strong arms and legs displayed wicked scars that spoke volumes. A thick leather belt circled his narrow waste, holding a well-used scabbard and sword. Simple leather sandals shod his feet. He appeared neither old nor young, but appearance was deceptive with true Council members. Kon-r had already lived eighty strenuous years, and, if he escaped violent death, he could expect to double or triple that number.

Kon-r smiled; his life would be cut dramatically short. The gods were laughing at his expense. Kon-r had a profound effect on people, much more so than his physical appearance dictated. He exuded an aura of quiet power and confidence. People felt better around him, about themselves and life in general. Everything seemed clearer when Kon-r was there. He knew this. He enjoyed his gift. And that was why the gods were laughing at him. For the first time in his life, he couldn't help his people when they desperately needed him.

The high peak of Creogh Radahar was located in the Westron Range of mountains that extended from north to south along the entire western coast of Athlan. The mountains rose steeply from the sea, reaching heights where the air became difficult to breathe. The peak was blasted flat: treeless, hard, barren. Kon-r, looking east, surveyed the tortured landscape below—his country, his responsibility. He lowered his head and closed his eyes. He was tired. In his mind, he saw the burned villages and collapsed buildings destroyed by the quakes. He saw canals flood, their levees broken beyond repair. He saw the ravaged plains and wondered what people would eat.

Athlaneans had always survived nature's challenges. In spite of the occasional natural calamity, they had continued to live productive, happy lives. This time, though, resistance to despair was failing. More citizens were accepting the inevitability of their destruction. Friendships were torn apart. Families disintegrated as members disappeared into smoke and flames. The people had lost the concept of the good fight. They had lost their self-respect. For Kon-r, helplessly watching his people unconditionally surrender to chaos was the ultimate defeat.

He knew the end was near when the Athlanean Council began to dissolve in his sixtieth year. The Council, originally formed in the unknowable past, had consisted of four members: the Priest, the Scientor, the Poet, and the Warrior. These four, usually but not always men, had directed the political and religious affairs of Athlan for as long as history had been recorded. The Four met on a regular basis to decide all serious matters of state—foreign and domestic—and create the policies that had kept Athlan safe and prosperous. The secret to their success had been balance. The Priest and Poet provided a good counterbalance to the Scientor and Warrior.

Public policy had remained remarkably stable over the centuries. Common sense and a desire to protect the people ruled the day—and always had. While the four Council designations remained the same, the people who held these seats changed as death claimed each of them. Replacements were not voted on, nor were they appointed. When replacements were needed, they were identified by special markings that appeared on their bodies. The remaining Council members had nothing to do with the selection process. No Council seat had ever been left vacant due to a member's death. Whether death was caused by disease or violence, whether it happened at home or abroad, a replacement always appeared promptly. The person who replaced the Priest found a sunburst pattern burned into the palm of his left hand. The next Poet was marked by the image of a red heart on the right palm. The new Scientor would awaken one day to find perfectly formed geometric symbols on the inside of his left forearm, and the new Warrior would wonder how an open hand, palm out, came to be on his left forearm, while a clenched fist adorned his right one. Over time, Council markings became accepted as a regular occurrence of nature. The tradition of "marking" became ordinary; it was taken for granted. The appearance of Council marks fell from the realm of the awesome to the mundane. Something significant had been lost.

Council members embodied the essence of their offices. They represented the best their society had to offer; some would say they were more than human. The Priest embodied moral principles and socially responsible behavior. He aggressively fought evil and despair. The Poet saw into the collective soul of the Athlaneans. He knew the truth of his people and tried to show them who they were and what they could be. These days, people no longer had the courage to peer into the mirror conjured by his words. His truths had become barbs.

The Scientor dealt in physical truths. His job was to know the material world and, through that knowledge, to make life better for the people. His devotion to science was interpreted by the masses as a means of denying anything that was not hard, physical fact. It was easier to believe the Scientor than it was the Priest or Poet.

The Warrior provided a haven for Athlanean society to prosper and grow. The Warrior borrowed the passion of the Poet, the dedication of the Priest, and the thirst for physical knowledge that defined the Scientor. The Warrior also possessed an indomitable will that drove his actions.

Kon-r was the Warrior of the age, and he was the last living Council member. He had been marked with the palm and fist in his twenty-second year, when the previous Warrior had succumbed to his wounds in an obscure battle far from home. Kon-r had killed the Priest himself. The Priest, whose name was Sagart, realized that he was paying far too much attention to the forms of his belief, while he lost his true focus—the promotion of faith and hope through good works. He began to revel in his power over frightened and helpless Athlaneans who, faced with death, began to turn to the gods of their ancestors, which meant they beseeched Sagart for salvation—physical and spiritual. As Sagart flourished in his new-found power, he also lost the spark of faith and slipped from the rock of humility. Kon-r met Sagart on the peak of Radahar and did the Poet's job—he held up a mirror to Sagart and confronted him, decrying his lack of true faith and his total loss of humility. Sagart, faced with the truth of his behavior, crumbled to the ground, and he begged Kon-r to end his life. Kon-r passed his sword through Sagart's heart, as if doing him a favor. No replacement came forth.

The Scientor, Eolicht, enjoyed the accolades of the people, who realized that their wealth was mainly due to his efforts. He spoke his mind, and the people of Athlan listened. He became convinced, however, that mankind was simply another type of physical existence, like animals or vegetables. Acts that had once been socially forbidden became habit.

The Poet, Cas Amhran, in a fit of frustrated rage, killed Eolicht because the cult of science was killing the soul of the Athlan people. In a true murder of passion, Cas Amhran choked the life out of Eolicht and threw his corpse from the heights of Creogh Radahar. A slight, refined-looking man with curly brown hair and light eyes, Cas was horrified by his own actions. The last of the great Poets, Cas Amhran realized his own failure and cried tears of anguish as he cast himself over the edge. Neither the red heart nor the perfect patterns were replaced.

As the Council disintegrated, earthquakes erupted on a regular basis. Cities were torn apart, villages leveled. Fires destroyed what was left of the Athlanean capitol, Cathair, erasing millennia of history and lives uncounted. Disease, unchecked and virulent, thinned the populace. The numerous canals on the Great Plain were being torn asunder by seismic pressure. The Plain was flooding; great rents in the earth split the island. Athlaneans, turned feral, searched for food—anything that would help them get through one more harrowing night.

Kon-r recognized the dual destruction of country and soul, one coin with two sides. He believed he was the last of the Council for one reason: he could not give up. That was the central axiom for the Warrior. He couldn't think himself into paralysis. He couldn't think himself into despair. He wasn't clever enough to rationalize another role for himself, and he wasn't coward enough to run away. He was trapped by his own character. Kon-r had resigned himself to fighting against two deadly enemies: nature and the destroyers of his home. He would do what he could.

He remembered discussions with Sagart, the Priest, before he became corrupted. Kon-r always felt more secure after listening to him explain the universe, the Angeals, and his role in the larger picture. The Priest had been so certain; he spoke so well. Kon-r wanted to believe, but when he was in the field with his men—the Marfach Gardei, the deadly guard—spiritual thoughts vanished, replaced by the need to survive, kill, and win. Wading through fresh battlefields amid the stench and sound of the dead and dying, Kon-r could never wrap his mind around the concept of an all-powerful, benevolent being.

Sitting atop Creogh Radahar, sea wind blowing through his black hair, Kon-r Sighur considered the latest bit of news that had reached him. A youth had been found, the son of a fisherman, bearing the marks of the Warrior. There had never been two Warriors at the same time, just like there had never been two Priests, two Scientors, or two Poets. But another Warrior seemed to exist. Why? Athlan was exploding into the sea. Should Kon-r train him to die with the rest of them in a fiery conflagration signifying nothing, to slide beneath the waves into oblivion, fully trained and completely useless?

Kon-r continued to brood over the double-Warrior dilemma. The only reason to train a new Warrior would be to send him out into the world, hoping he could carry on the Warrior tradition. How could he possibly prepare a new Warrior for the chaos of a future world?

Kon-r saw the insidious nature of despair; he doubted his own worth. Fighting against insurmountable odds defined his role. Resistance against evil was necessary, because victory was never assured, and when victory was achieved, it was, by nature, a temporary reprieve: evil always returned. He decided the boy Warrior would be tested, and, if he passed, he would be trained as thoroughly as time allowed. He would be sent away before the final collapse. The new Warrior would carry on. Maybe tradition would change as the world changed, or maybe he would perish. Either way, one more Warrior might enter the world. It was all Kon-r could do. Perhaps it was all he was ever meant to do. He laughed. As black as things were becoming, he laughed because no matter how deeply he tried to think these things through, it never mattered. He could never get the solid, concrete answers he could understand. It was all a mystery, as Sagart used to say piously. Kon-r kept on laughing, convinced that the mystery was more like a bad joke.

chapter 2:

SUMMONS

Cean Mak-Scaire, the son of a fisherman, had received a summons to appear before Kon-r Sighur, the last Warrior of the destroyed Council. The message had been delivered by an officer of the Marfach Gardei, who made it crystal clear to Cean that if he didn't appear at the appointed hour, he would be caught and dragged before the Warrior. Cean had little formal education, but he was far from stupid. Cean wondered why the marks of the Warrior stained his arms. Kon-r wasn't dead. There could never be two Warriors at once, and, because of this, he expected to be put to death. Anger welled in his heart, not fear. Why should he die for something he was not responsible for? With Cathair crumbling around him, Cean decided that he would go to the Ban Castlean and live.

Cean was larger than most of his friends, but not exceptionally so—there were plenty of bigger men along the docks. He learned at an early age that he could play any game and play it well. He was unbeatable. He could wrestle, but boxing was his favorite. His hands moved faster than the eye could follow. Opponents' heads snapped back as if pulled by gossamer strings, and people were always astonished to see blood splatter and eyes swell shut, as if struck by invisible blows. He never fought angry, nor did he try to hurt people. To him, all matches were sport. Playful competition was to him as it was to a cub, who naively sharpened its survival skills in play.

As he aged, though, Cean no longer looked for friendly contests of skill. The devastation of Athlan had touched him deeply when his mother and father had died in the collapse of their simple waterfront home. Cean had sifted through the rubble, looking for something to remember them by. He found precious little—a singed blanket, a short knife, a bloody sandal—those were the relics of his past. He vowed never to forget his parents. He didn't get to say goodbye to them. He felt so alone with the damned marks on his arms.

Raven-black hair framed a strong, smooth face dominated by glowing blue eyes. His blemish-free skin was tanned from a life outdoors. He wore no beard and could not grow one if he tried. Tall and strong, when Cean flashed his white teeth in a smile, everyone around him felt his joy as their own. Athlan girls were drawn to Cean. Yet he was not conscious of his effect on them. They simply weren't very important to him in the sense that he didn't need them for anything. He was content to take care of himself. And, since the death of his parents, this trait had stood him in good stead. People wanted to follow Cean, but he had no desire to lead.

He had been told to report to Kon-r Sighur on the peak of Creogh Radahar by noon two days hence. He ran steadily, avoiding the gangs of men that roamed through the detritus of great Cathair. He ran past women offering themselves for a coin or a bit of food. The dead lay in doorways and gutters. Packs of wild dogs mauled indefinable flesh that may have once been human. He ran through clouds of rancid smoke, trying to ignore the smells of destruction. Cean wore a light-brown tunic belted with a slender cord. He carried the knife from home in a sheath strapped to his forearm. His sandaled feet slapped the ancient cobblestones as he picked up the pace, trying to get through the nightmare of Cathair as fast as possible.

He turned down an alley that looked like it might be a promising shortcut. The narrow alley became choked with smoke; he couldn't see, and before he could stop, he ran into a man who blocked his path. The man grunted and stepped back, but Cean bounced backwards and lay dazed on the cobblestones. The stranger was very large, bald, and bleeding. His left eye was a memory of better times. He laughed as Cean staggered to his feet, but it was not a pleasant sound.

"There you are, young fisherman. I have been searching for you. People are interested in your life and have paid me to take it." He staggered towards Cean, raising his sword to strike. Cean grabbed his short knife and threw it into the mercenary's remaining eye. The soldier froze, put both of his hands over his face, screamed once, and fell like an ancient, lightening-blasted oak. He landed on his back, his lifeless hands and arms flung out, touching both alley walls. Cean cautiously approached the body, curious about his first kill. He had never thrown a knife before and couldn't remember thinking about doing it. He had just done it. He plucked the knife from the bleeding socket and wiped it clean on the man's tunic.

The man's armor was old and beat up, but his sword lay in the street, softly glowing. Cean bent to pick it up. As he grasped the sword, it felt hot. He was stunned by a vision of a large figure wreathed in flames and wearing black armor that pointed a flaming sword of death at his heart. Cean grabbed the real sword in both hands, stumbling away from the body, but could not drop the hot weapon. His hands shook. He sensed tremendous power in both the sword and the vision. He had seen this vision before, and many others since the marks had become visible, but never like this. This was more than a dream. He looked at the weapon again. It was almost three feet long and sharpened along both edges. The point was a needle. There seemed to be some type of writing engraved in the blade that he couldn't make out. Cean gripped the leather-wrapped pommel and watched as the grooves in the wrapping adjusted themselves to match his fingers. The guard was made of serpentine circles of some unknown metal that formed an intricate metallic lace arm. The pommel ended with a ball of heavy metal, and Cean instinctively knew that anyone hit with that ball would never get back up. He took the scabbard and belt from the dead man, slid the sword in, and looped the belt over his back. He felt very different with this unwholesome weapon. Whatever was happening to him was not comforting. Cean felt like he was being pushed, herded like a dumb animal, and he didn't like it. Who was this man, and who wanted him dead? He continued to run through Cathair's living burial grounds.

chapter 3:

GO AND LIVE

Cean stood before the main gate of the Ban Castlean, the Ivory Castle, chest heaving, eyes bright. Pushed by some otherworldly force, he had run for two days and nights to arrive on time. The walls were massive and carved with runes. The rock of the fortress was white, glowing in the sunlight, on an island nation where all other rock was hard, black basalt. There was no explanation. The entire castle was carved from the living rock of Radahar. The only breach in the natural stone was the main gate, which was made of black basalt and twelve feet thick. The stone swung on pinballs of gran-steel and, when closed, long, thick bars of gran-steel slid into place along the top, middle, and bottom sections of the gate. The Ban Castlean had never been broken.

Cean was terribly excited. He began walking toward the massive gateway. Covered in sweat, he was smiling, a good-natured peasant boy on a great adventure. An arrow, fletched red, whistled through the air and, quivering, struck the ground before his feet. He jumped back and pulled out his new sword. Another arrow landed behind him. The huge gate opened soundlessly. Three men walked out. Each was a member of the Marfach Gardei, armed with sword, bow, and short killing spear. Cean gripped his sword tighter and shouted, "I am Cean Mak-Scaire. I have been summoned by Kon-r Sighur. Who are you?"

The triad marched closer to Cean and stopped. The soldier in the center of the line took two steps forward, well within striking range, and answered: "I am Donal Mac Beir. I am the Master Sergeant of the Marfach Gardei and gatekeeper of Ban Castlean. We have followed Kon-r into battle for more than twenty solar cycles. You shall not pass."

Cean looked into Donal's eyes and knew he meant what he said. "I don't understand. Kon-r himself summoned me. You must know this. Why do you stand in my way?"

Donal adjusted his stance. He answered, "Turn and walk away. You will live. Advance, and you die. There can be only one Warrior. Our world dies, but the Marfach Gardei will not abandon Kon-r."

"I didn't come to kill anyone!" Cean shouted. He lifted his arms, exposing the marks. "I don't know what it all means. I beg you, let me pass. I am summoned."

"Are you deaf, boy? You will not pass. Defend yourself." Donal Mac Beir, renowned centurion, battle-hardened veteran, swept to attack. Cean instinctively shifted his weight, brought his sword up over his right shoulder, stepped his left foot out with knees slightly bent, and waited. Donal was on him in a flash, and the sword strikes came from all angles. Cean moved intuitively. He could see Donal's intent a fraction of a second before each attack. They danced in the sun. The other two men did not move. Cean knew that Donal's speed was no match for his own. Just as Cean was beginning to feel confident in the outcome of this battle, Donal whirled and brought the blade up from his knees and slashed Cean with a vertical stroke, cutting his stomach and chest and slicing the tip of his chin. But the cut wasn't a death blow. Cean's tunic fell away, and a line of blood appeared. He stepped back in shock and looked into Donal's eyes. "You are fast, but not skilled," Donal warned, "and you are not immortal. Go and live, for I sense no cowardice in you. But you shall not pass, and if you stay, you will die."

Something changed in Cean then. He stood still, sword in hand, feet slightly apart. He looked at these men; he saw the sky and the wall before him. This was no longer a game, and he was no longer a boy. Donal had forced him to come to grips with himself. He could not walk away. He had to stand and fight. Donal would have to die, because Donal wouldn't back down. Cean said, "I cannot back away. I know what you are, and I respect you. Please, let me pass."

Donal saw the determination in Cean's eyes. "This one is dangerous. This one could be a fine soldier. Perhaps he would be the Warrior, but not on Donal Mac Beir's watch." Donal looked straight into his eyes. "I see you, Cean, and I know you. Still, you will not pass while I draw breath." Donal attacked. He increased his effort. Stamp and stab, stamp and stab, slash the eyes, slice down low—slash the legs, whirl and reverse, hack from above, shoulder into chest, push and lunge.

Donal didn't feel the cut. His eyes followed as Cean backed away, and he looked perplexed, as if he wondered why Cean wasn't standing in front of him, ready to receive what Donal thought would be the final strike. "Why, What..." He crumbled to his knees, watching his own blood dripping onto the sand. Donal clasped his cold hands over the wound, trying to keep his entrails within his ravaged body. His sword lay on the bloody ground, forgotten. The soldier on the right stepped behind Donal and drew his blade, whispering to his centurion, listening to his faint answer. Donal slowly raised his head. He focused on Cean's face. "I am but the first. You fought well. Perhaps you are the one. I, I...have been found insufficient for this task...." Talking became difficult for him. "I...kept...my...vow." The standing Gardei officer's blade whistled as it slashed. Donal's head remained in place for a moment, and his eyes blinked once as his head fell to the earth.

Cean let out a deep sigh. He had killed a man who wanted to kill him. It was that simple. He had killed a skilled warrior and had felt comfortable doing it. But the moves and the swordplay—where had they come from? He had no training, and Donal had been a master. Cean was a fisherman's son no longer. He checked the other Gardei, but they made no moves against him. Other soldiers were streaming out of the gate, and Cean set his feet for more battles, but those men hurried to Donal's side and carried the body into the citadel. One man approached Cean, who remained ready to fight. "I am Silidar Kormac, centurion and friend of Donal. I come not to fight, but to direct you. Go through the main gate and bear right, up the paved street. It is called the Path of Endurance. Eventually, if this is your fate, that street will take you to the Warrior."

Cean looked at the centurion and sensed that he, too, was ready to challenge him. "Will I meet others who want to take my life on this journey up the mountain?" Cean asked.

The centurion looked directly into his eyes and answered, "You may. Life is not an open book. We are all dedicated to Kon-r. I do not challenge you here and now because I was ordered not to, but have no doubt—each of these men would try to kill you if allowed. You are anathema to our beliefs. You should not exist, and you will not threaten Kon-r." He stepped aside and said abruptly, "Go to your fate." Cean watched the honor guard carry Donal's dead form through the gates, sheathed his sword on his back, gave Silidar Kormac a look of defiance, and trotted toward the gate. Cean was looking forward to his trials, and this knowledge more than anything made him realize he was no longer the boy who ran away from home to answer a summons.He was a man, maybe more than a man, going to meet his destiny.

Chapter 4:

TRANSFORMATION

Toward the center of burning Cathair, clouded in smoke, another rite was taking place beneath a temple long ignored by Athlaneans. The temple once served the ancient god of retribution, Graxas, but was pulled down when that god was declared dead by the Council of Four. Devotion to Graxas never died completely, however, and the beliefs of his cult had mutated over the years from a god of revenge into a god that fed on hatred, bloodshed, and fear. Graxas had become the face of an ancient evil that had always plagued the world by many names. Its primary purpose had always been, and still was, to oppose every positive action by the Council of Four.

The room was large but low. Squat black pillars lined the walls. Torches illuminated the corners, and dark, greasy smoke coated the ceiling. Shadows flickered across scores of armed men who edged the room. Their faces were wrapped in black cloth; only their eyes showed in the wavering light. Two men occupied the center of the room. One stood in a hooded black robe, face wrapped in black, and the other, dressed in the same black robe but with his face exposed, knelt before him. They were whispering to each other.

The standing man was old; his hands were wrinkled and bent. His hair, where it escaped from his hood, was wispy and white. His eyes, however, shone red in the dim light, as if they generated a heat of their own. His cowled face was parched and wrinkled, but sharp as glass: all angles and planes. There was no mercy in that face, no love. He was called the Bas Mor, the Great Death; if he had ever had another name, it was long since forgotten. He was the high priest of Graxas. He worked in the shadows and sowed discontent wherever he or his minions traveled. He brought strife and bloodshed. He replaced faith and hope with doubt and despair. He was the negative force in the world and the sworn enemy of the Council, as were the high priests of Graxas before him.

The Bas Mor raised his hands over his head and showed his palms to every man in the room. The left displayed a red dragon and the right a black one. The men along the walls stamped their feet and clashed their weapons; they screamed nightmarish blood oaths as the Bas Mor completed his demonstration. He faced the kneeling youth once more and continued to whisper. The young man stared intensely into those red, inhuman eyes. Their faces began to pull together, as if drawn by invisible bands of power. The youth stood, the same height as his mentor. He was well built and good to look on. Dark hair framed his face. His eyes were pale blue, although now they reflected the burning red of the Bas Mor. His name was Pian, and he didn't know it, but he looked disturbingly like the Bas Mor had when he was the same age. In fact, he mirrored a long line of priests that looked disquietingly alike in the service of Graxas.

The Bas Mor's voice rolled and echoed like thunder in the enclosed chamber. He held out his marked palms, and Pian pressed his palms to those of his master, joining old with new. "Now, Pian, do you swear by Graxas, under pain of death and eternal suffering, that you will assume the responsibilities of the Bas Mor of Graxas in this time of death and destruction?"

"I do."

"Do you swear to continue the rites of Graxas even after the destruction of Athlan?"

"I do."

"Do you swear to work ceaselessly for the destruction of mankind wherever and whenever you can, as demanded by Graxas, your eternal savior?"

"I do."

"Finally, do you swear to continue the line of Graxas's High Priests when your time comes to an end?"

"I do."

"Athlan will shortly be no more. No more will the Marfach Gardei thwart our plans. They, like the island itself, will be dead. No more will the Warrior, or any warrior, come against us in this world. We are now free to work our will." Throughout his oration, the armed men in the chamber howled and stamped their feet; the heat in the chamber intensified as the group worked itself into a frenzy. They moved away from the wall, closing in on the sacred pair.

The Bas Mor lowered his voice to deliver his instructions. "When I am gone and you have assumed command, you must attack the Marfach Gardei. You must destroy them here, on Athlan, before you go. They must not follow you. Each man in this room commands a large body of trained fighters. Through them, you command an army of more than ten thousand fanatics dedicated to the Gardei's destruction."

Pian answered quickly, "Yes, master, but how are we to breach the walls of the Ban Castlean?"

The Bas Mor's hand moved like a snake and locked on Pian's throat, cutting off his air supply. "Do you doubt me, boy? Have you learned nothing? Am I leaving this earth in the hands of a coward, or worse, an idiot?" He removed his hand and left Pian gasping for breath. "We have a man—Fealtoir—who deserted the Gardei years ago. We have questioned him and learned much of the Gardei and their stronghold. There exists a sea cave on the western shore, cut low into the rock, that leads to the ancient sewers of the castle. This path has been unused for thousands of years. Fealtoir revealed that it could be followed into the citadel. We sent him in with simple instructions: find the way in or die. He still lives. I have devised a two-pronged attack that will allow you to use the cave unnoticed. In the next months, spread the word that the Marfach Gardei is hoarding food and ships that will allow them to escape while everyone else dies. When the people are whipped into a fighting frenzy, insert some of your commanders into the crowd to send them against the gates. The death count does not matter. If none gain entry, it does not matter. The only thing that matters is that they stay before the gates and keep the attention of the Gardei, while you and your force slip through the cave into the city.

You will do this at night. You will lead, but you will not fight. Once inside the fort, the Warrior must be killed. The entire attack is aimed at killing the Warrior. Do you understand?" The Great Death took a large roll of parchment from his robe. "Fealtoir drew this map for us. The Warrior's rooms are clearly marked. While your force attacks the garrison, you will lead a group of your best men. At-az, my loyal captain, can pick them, no fewer than one hundred, and you will seek out and kill the Warrior. Do you understand?"

"Yes."

"So be it." The Bas Mor gazed into Pian's eyes for what seemed an eternity. "Tell me, Pian, are you having dreams?"

"Yes, master, I am."

"And are they pleasant?"

"No, master, they are not. I frequently dream about flying among the stars, and a giant wind sweeps me from the sky. I fall and fall, and as I fall, I burn and the wind fans the fires. And I scream, and others are burning and screaming around me; and we fall into darkness in pain, burning..." There was real anguish in Pian's eyes as he remembered. "What does it mean, master?"

The Bas Mor smiled a death's head grin, as he saw the worry in his protégé's eyes. "That dream has been dreamt by every high priest of

Graxas since the beginning. We think, we believe—we do not know—that we are the servants of those burning beings who fell. We believe that one is supreme—Graxas—and you and I are the latest of his high priests. We believe that the Warrior is and always has been the earthly defender of the power that cast Graxas down so many ages ago. We fight for command of this planet, and our time grows near."

They joined palms, and their hands shimmered, as if a great heat was generated by the coupling. Pian gasped; the pain became excruciating. A transfer was taking place. As he stared into those ancient eyes, Pian saw the Bas Mor's life. He saw all that the Bas Mor had accomplished for his god. He saw the frustration that Graxas had suffered at the hands of the Marfach Gardei and the Four. Pian learned the history of his order—the victories and defeats, the progression of battles, the secret growth of the cult—and he smiled through the pain. He smiled because he saw what the Bas Mor knew: they were winning the war for the hearts and souls of people all over the world. Faith and hope were being crushed and once the steadying hand of Athlan was no more, the world had an excellent opportunity to destroy itself. Graxas would be served.

The Bas Mor knew what was happening to Pian. The same had happened to him many years earlier. Pian was his creation. Once an innocent boy from a nondescript farm, despair had taken over and sacrificed his mind and soul to bloodthirsty purposes. Despair almost laughed as the Bas Mor remembered degrading the boy year after year, one instance only slightly more serious than the last—killing a small animal, followed by a larger one, then hurting a child, and then more seriously wounding a baby, and so on. It had been so much fun for the Bas Mor to watch an innocent boy become totally warped, eventually enjoying it, embracing the corruption as normal. That was the ultimate perversion that described the young man who now stood in front of him. The Bas Mor had done his job.

"Pian, are you ready to assume your responsibilities?"

"Yes, master."

"Have you looked into my life? Have you seen the past through my eyes?"

"Yes, master."

"Do you understand the true nature of the struggle we are engaged in?"

"Yes, master, I do: we fight to strengthen our god through the perversion of humanity. We fight to bring him dominion of the earth, and we will rule in his name. We must destroy the Warrior, the Marfach Gardei, and any who come after them. We will operate behind the thrones of power, manipulating those who obey it. Finally, I must choose and train a successor, as you chose and trained me. Do I understand, master?"

"You do." The Bas Mor looked around the chamber one more time and smiled grimly. It was good. He had done his best. There was one final thing to say. "Pian, when I am gone, and you have destroyed the Warrior, take as many brethren as you can from this island. Keep them close. You will need protection. You will need men to do your bidding. In time, you will find new converts to our faith. Kill the Warrior and be gone. Let no one know where you are headed. Do you swear to do this?"

"I do, master."

The Bas Mor nodded. The brethren were within arm's reach of the pair. Each man had a weapon in his hand. Their eyes gleamed in the half-light, their mouths open, panting in the tremendous heat. The Bas Mor said, "Get ready. It will hurt. Are you ready?" Pian nodded, eager for the pain. "So be it." The Bas Mor clasped Pian's hands tightly in his, palm to palm, and began to force his tremendous energy, his indomitable will to destroy, his hate, his fear, his disgust with all things human into Pian's body and mind. Both men seemed to grow. Their eyes glowed feral red. Both screamed as if their bodies were being torn apart and burned to ash. The brethren backed away from the conflagration. They fell over one another trying to escape that which they did not understand. The Bas Mor continued to fill Pian with his memories, which were his and also those of every high priest who had come before. Their bodies were now wrapped in a red cloud of power. They shimmered before the brethren, insubstantial, seeming to become one, fused beyond comprehension. The brethren dropped to their knees and screamed as tortured animals. The sound reverberated in the stone chamber and became a physical force as the heat of their coupling grew beyond endurance. A final thunderclap ended the rite.

Pian collapsed to his knees. The old man shrunk to his knees, too, and then toppled over onto the stone floor, dead and withered. His face was a desiccated skull, his body a stick figure lost in its voluminous robe. Pian raised his head, and those who could see gasped. Pian's face was also a skull, but as they watched, flesh and hair emerged to cover it. The eyes opened, and they were red, and the face was the same aged face of the Bas Mor. Pian saw the shocked expressions of his followers, and he laughed. He knew the world would bleed at his command. Pian held up his hands, palms outward, and there were the black and red dragons burnt into each palm. The commanders clashed their weapons and knelt in silence. The young man once called Pian addressed his commanders. "I am the Bas Croi—Death Heart—and we will be the death of all that the Council of Four has wrought in this world. Will you come and kill with me?" The commanders created such a noise that the stone walls shook on their foundations. Evil lived in that chamber. The transformation was complete. Graxas would be well-served again.

chapter 5:

OTHERS

Cean jogged through the main gate and ran down the tunnel toward the inner gate. He felt trapped and isolated. The second gate, called the Cruel Gate, did not open for him, and Cean thought he would certainly die there. He stood looking straight ahead, as if he was willing the gate open. He became angry. His blue eyes blazed in defiance. This was no game. A good man was dead already. After a few silent seconds, he held up his forearms for all to see, slowly moving his arms from left to right, and shouted, "I am Cean Mak-Scaire! I carry the marks of the Warrior, and I have been summoned by Kon-r Sighur! Who blocks my way? What cowards lurk behind this gate? Open! Face me!" Cean surprised himself. Where had that attitude come from? The gate began to rise.

Cean saw that there was no one on the other side. No one waited to wage battle. He began to walk through the Cruel Gate. He entered a large, octagonal courtyard. A low fountain bubbled in the center of the plaza. There were no doors visible. Cean knew he had to move to his right and up, but he couldn't see a road or path. He stood confused, suspecting the worst, when he heard a voice in front of him. "Lost, boy?" Cean located the voice; he saw an old man, or was it an old woman, sitting on the edge of the fountain. Its hair was white, as was its beard, both of which blended into the bubbling water behind him, and its tunic blended into the fountain stones perfectly. The eyes were as blue as Cean's and just as clear. Cean approached, confident that the apparition posed no danger.

"Hello, could you tell me how to find the...?"

"You want to know how to find the Path of Endurance. Is that it, young Warrior?" "Yes, it is. How did you know? And why did you call me Warrior?"

The translucent being chuckled, its low laughter magnifying the sounds of the fountain. "There are many things on this earth that you do not know, Cean. I am one of those things." Cean was no longer sure that he was as safe as he had thought.

"And what are you, if you don't mind my asking?"

An old woman smiled. Her answer was slow in coming. "What am I? Not an easy question to answer. I am many things to many people.

For now, all you need to know is this: I have been appointed to watch over you in certain situations."

Cean asked, "Is this one of those situations?"

"No, Cean, it is not. I thought I would take this time to introduce myself. My most common name is...."

Cean couldn't hear the name. "Could you say your name again?"

The woman moved her lips, but Cean still couldn't hear the name. "I can't hear your name."

A smile appeared again on the old woman's face. "I know. Nor will you hear my name until you earn the right."

Cean asked, "Can the others here see you?"

"No, Cean, they cannot."

"Are you of this world?"

An old man nodded appreciatively, "Yes and no, son. I am more natural to the heavens than I am to earth. I can act only in special situations, situations that may be beyond your ability to understand."

Cean was getting seriously worried. "Who forbids your actions? And why can't they see you? And how did you get here? Does Kon-r....?" By this time, the old man was laughing hard, so hard that his cackles echoed across the plaza. Later, members of the Marfach Gardei would tell stories about the day the plaza shook and the fountain soared, the day Cean Mak-Scaire first exercised his power.

"Enough. Your path lies behind that wall. You will find your path."

"Will we meet again?"

"We may, Cean. I believe we will, although you may not recognize our meeting; but even if we do not, I will always be aware of you and your enemies wherever you go."

Cean was more puzzled than ever. *What enemies?* he thought. Walking away, he turned to ask, "Who...?"

The old man, or old woman, had vanished. It had been that kind of day. Cean followed the instructions and regained his path.

As he walked up the Path of Endurance, Cean saw homes and shops cut into the rock. Each door was a different shade of faded paint. There was writing carved into the lintels above most doors, but Cean couldn't read the script. Some of the buildings were empty. The streets were quiet. Cean saw people moving ahead of him, and occasionally he saw a face in a window. He was a stranger, and he felt his isolation.

Cean continued to walk, now in shade, now in light, and his steps were heavy as he felt the weight of a history unknown. The marks on his arms connected him to this history. He looked ahead and saw that the path was doubling back across the face of Creogh Radahar, angling up the mountain face. Facing the sun, the road brightened. The interior became an oven as the sun's light and heat reflected off building walls and stone streets. Cean had to keep his head down. The light was too bright. He looked sideways and slightly forward, as people must when walking into the sun. The path widened in front of him. Squinting, his hand shading his eyes, Cean saw that he had entered a small, beautiful square, and in the center of the square, there was a tall statue. The figure was bright white, brilliant in the sun. Cean could not look directly at it. He began to move away when a cloud passed overhead, briefly shading the sculpture. Cean looked up again and let out an alarmed shout, lost his balance, and landed hard on the stones of the path. He was stunned.

Before him was the form of... what, a man? A man with twelve wings sprouting from his back, whose long, beautifully carved hair flowed in the wind, a man with simple robes and sandaled feet, holding a glowing sword pointed over the horizon, and an open, empty left hand. The face was stern, handsome with chiseled features and piercing eyes. Cean felt the force of those eyes; he could sense the power in this being. This image was another that had haunted him since the marks appeared. Cean approached the statue. He put his hand on the figure's foot. It was cool to the touch; he backed away, looking up at the eyes one more time. He walked around the figure, and as he did so, he thought he saw the statue's eyes follow him. He didn't look up again. He shivered in fear and resumed his course. The eyes had moved. He would never tell anyone, but they had. He ran.

The path was like an oven. Sweat poured from his body, soaking his tunic, burning his eyes. He continued to run, feeling firm muscles beneath his taut skin, feeling his lungs labor to draw huge drafts of heated air. This was living; this he understood. Head down, body leaning into the slope, arms pumping in short, powerful thrusts, Cean eventually found himself standing on a flat, sandy surface in a large square. The sun still obscured his vision. He walked across the sand, breathing heavily, hands on his hips, head thrown back, eyes narrowed against the light. He was out of breath but was not in pain. This was, in fact, pleasant. He could feel the sand burning the sides of his feet; he could feel the heat rising from the earth. He felt good, and then he heard "Stop!"

chapter 6:

CHOICE

The voice was close and commanding. Cean continued to walk forward as he put his hand over his eyes. A lithe, well-built man of Cean's same height stood in front of him. He wore nothing but a shimmering mail girdle. He held a long, shafted weapon in front of him with both hands. At one end, Cean could see a wickedly curved blade. At the other was a large ball, just larger than his impressive fist, studded with spikes. The man began to twirl his weapon with both hands. It moved faster and faster until Cean thought he was looking at a solid wall of flickering metal. The man and his swirling sword began to walk toward Cean, who drew his sword from its worn scabbard and took a ready stance. The man circled his weapon over his head and around his body in an intimidating display, and then he stopped. Two other men were positioned next to their leader, two paces back, forming a triangle. Cean's time had come again.

"My name is Craic Morn, centurion of the Marfach Gardei. I, like Donal before me, am here to kill you, unless you leave the Ban Castlean now. You shall not pass." Cean studied the man. He was younger than Donal by far, but still older than Cean. He was sleek and muscular, light on his feet. He moved through the sand easily. He was strong, and his endurance had to be assumed. Sweat glistened on his body. This man was in his element. His eyes glittered darkly and sent a message of death.

"I am Cean Mak-Scaire. I have no quarrel with you. I had none with Donal. I have been summoned to the peak of Creogh Radahar by Kon-r Sighur, and I will keep that appointment."

Morn took a step forward. "You will not." As he said these words, a whistle filled the air and another weapon to match Morn's stuck into the sand on Cean's right side. Where it had come from, he couldn't tell, but he knew that this was to be a fair fight. He could have easily been dead by now. "Drop your sword. We will fight as equals. The weapon is called a katal. Mine is called Life Stealer. It is an ancient and deadly design."

Cean didn't know whether this was a good idea. But he had to prove his superiority. He grabbed the bottom of his tunic and cut a three-inch swath from the lower edge. He tossed the knife down and tied the cloth around his head, knotting it tightly in the back. Now his hair was secure, and sweat would not run into his eyes. He grabbed his katal with both hands as Morn did. He was amazed by its lightness. He tossed it from hand to hand, feeling the balance, and he instinctively knew how and where to grip it. Morn was right: it was a deadly weapon.

Morn attacked. The battle was on. Cean didn't know what to do, but he knew he couldn't stand still. He held his weapon in front of him diagonally, blade up and right, ball low on the left. Morn began a rhythmic dance as he approached Cean, moving to his left, then his right, manipulating the katal in a hypnotic pattern, always closing the distance with his opponent. Morn's dance became a vicious attack, his double-edged blade jabbing straight at Cean's heart. The move was blindingly fast, and Cean barely deflected the blade. Cean never felt the curved edge as it sliced his flesh. He was too busy avoiding the spiked end of the Life Stealer as Morn tried to sweep Cean's legs out from under him. Cean leapt into the air to avoid the sweep, which was followed by a vertical strike aimed at the center of his head. Cean moved the katal in front of and over his head to block the move with the shaft of his weapon. When Cean blocked the strike, Morn moved back a pace, which let Cean find his balance as he landed in the sand.

"Well done, fisherman's son. Not many have experienced that sequence and lived. Ready to continue?"

Cean stood, breathing hard. His shoulder hurt and blood dripped onto the sand. He realized that he had probably taken Morn's best moves and was still standing. "I am ready, Craic Morn. I hope you have something better to show me. Defend yourself." Cean leaped forward, and what he lacked in skill, he made up for in speed and ferocity. He rained down blows from all angles. He cut Morn with a dozen slices that left the centurion bloody and confused. For his trouble, Cean suffered minor cuts on his hands and arms. Morn had dropped to his knees and was leaning on his weapon for support. Both men were breathing hard. Cean began to walk back and forth before his enemy, waiting for him to resume the fight.

Morn finally stood, still leaning on his katal. "You fight well, Mak-Scaire. The killing of Donal was no accident. I would gladly fight beside you in battle, but that will not change what must happen here. Are you ready to finish it?"

Cean stopped pacing. "We don't have to finish it. You are wound-ed. You are losing too much blood. Step aside and let me continue my journey. You lose no honor here."

Morn stepped forward with renewed energy. Anger blazed in his eyes. "Would you have me walk away from Donal's death? Do you think me craven? You have much to learn about men, Mak-Scaire, but you never will. Defend yourself." Craic Morn, weapons master of the Marfach Gardei, swung his Life Stealer, blade first, at Cean's eyes with incredible speed. Cean caught a flicker of reflected sunlight from the blade. Instead of moving back a step, he dropped to his knees and felt the wind on his face as Morn's blade flew over his head. As he fell, Cean swung the ball end of his katal into the extended right knee with all the force he could bring to bear. Morn's knee shattered, the sharp crack of broken bone as loud as his anguished scream. Cean charged Morn before he could get up. He knocked the Life Stealer from his hands with his own weapon and placed the double-edged blade against the hollow of Morn's throat.

Cean gently pushed the defeated Gardei down into the sand. "This battle is over. You don't have to die." Morn tried to force his body up, his throat pushing against the blade, which began to sink into the soft flesh. Cean realized Morn was trying to kill himself; he was trying to gain a warrior's death. Cean removed the blade from his throat. "Don't do this." Morn turned onto his stomach and began to crawl toward his katal. The other soldiers remained still.

Cean knelt and punched Morn on the back of the head. One punch rendered him senseless. Cean threw down his weapon and said to the nearest soldier, "Take him to a physician. He can be saved. Men like Craic Morn must be saved. He will hate me when he awakens, but tell him I would be happy to be his friend, if he would have me."

And if I make it through this day, he thought. Cean retrieved his weapons and began walking into the sun, his legs like jelly, his body drained. He had added scars and experience. He didn't know what to think, but he did know that a good man was not dead by his choice.

chapter 7:

BOUGHT AND SOLD

Pian sat in the darkness below the ruined Temple of Graxas. The small crypt was his throne room. He smiled. He wouldn't need the usual trappings of power. He would prove his strength in time. He realized that he thought of himself as the Bas Croi. Pian was no more—gone, as if he had never lived. This disturbed the Bas Croi, because it made him relive the time when he was found by the Bas Mor.

His name had been Pian, and he had been the third of five children born to Ancid and Sheboth Slithy. His father, Ancid, did odd work all over Athlan without a specific skill; he was gone most of the time. Pian's mother, Sheboth, suffered the life of a woman who had to do too many things for her family without sufficient resources. Throughout his childhood, Pian had watched her become quieter, more docile, less interested in everything around her. Pian, as a well-built boy of eight years, began to explore the area around his small home. No one watched him very closely. He found that he had an interest in small animals and what he could do to them. He also liked the idea that they could do very little to him. He tore them apart and then timed how long it took them to die. He stayed away from larger animals, like dogs or cats, because they could fight back. Pian had no stomach for these small but fierce battles. He soon tired of these games altogether, and he began roaming the village at night, looking through windows, listening outside open doors, trying to learn his neighbors' secrets. Property began to go missing, and people began to whisper about Pian. Other children shunned him, and the men and women of the village began to flash angry looks at Ancid and Sheboth, offering work to other men instead of Ancid. Pian didn't care. He was too clever to be caught, and no one could see what stolen knowledge he kept in his head. When questioned, even when slapped around, Pian would remain quiet, tormenting his tormentors with a smirk, which infuriated them.

One day, when Pian was ten, he saw his father entering their yard accompanied by a tall and thin man Pian didn't recognize. The man walked with a long, gnarled black staff capped at both ends with dull metal. His black robe dragged on the ground, and he wore a hood pulled over his head, even though it was a hot day. Pian noticed that his father kept looking back at the man who walked two paces behind him. His father looked nervous and frightened.

They stopped in front of Pian, and his father pointed to the boy and said, "That's him." The black-clad stranger approached Pian and told him to stand up. He did.

The stranger bent down and moved his face within inches of Pian's and said, "Come with me, boy, and I will teach you how to rule these cattle. You will learn their darkest secrets; you will be taught how to cause exquisite pain."

Pian looked into the eyes hidden within the darkness of the cowl. He saw raw pain; he saw hate and malice; he saw terror beyond imagination. He saw his future, and he said, "I will come."

The stranger answered, "I am the Bas Mor; you will call me master." The stranger turned to Pian's father, reached into his robe, and handed him a small pouch of coins. Ancid took the money and rushed into their house. After a few seconds, Pian heard his mother scream, but that was all: one scream. Pian and the Bas Mor walked out of the yard and down the road; neither looked back.

Over the years, Bas Mor proved to be a clever teacher. He played Pian like a fine instrument, fanning his desires, showing him how to cause pain, how to use the knowledge he stole, how to plan the downfall of others. Pian's unnatural appetites grew as he did. Larger animals died. People began to disappear from the countryside. Pian was experimenting and liking the work. Bas Mor sent him on missions across Athlan, as well as to other continents; his missions always involved death, mayhem, or the thievery of some secret item that was necessary for future actions. Pian never failed the Bas Mor. Pian was a natural. He passed every test the Bas Mor devised, tests the Bas Mor had also passed in his youth.

One day, as Pian was throwing knives at a target, Bas Mor said to him, "I have one final task for you, Pian. Do you ever think of your parents?"

Pian stopped mid-throw. "No, master, I don't."

"Would it interest you to know that they are both still alive, still living in the same house where you grew up?" Pian ran his fingers along the edge of one of the knives. Blood trickled down the blade, dripping to the ground.

Pian looked intently into the Bas Mor's red eyes. "Yes, it might, master." The Bas Mor could sense the boy's eagerness.

The Bas Mor continued, "Would you like to pay them a visit?"

Pian went rigid; he could hardly get the words out as he gasped, "Yes, yes, I would, master."

The Bas Mor nodded. "Return to me in three days with gifts."

Pian did a quarter turn and threw the knife as hard as he could. It struck the middle of the target and sunk up to the hilt. "Thank you, master. I will return in three days with gifts."

Three days later, the Bas Mor found two heads on the main alter of Graxas. Ancid and Sheboth Slithy were no more. Bas Mor had expected as much, but he didn't expect that the eyes and lips would be missing from the heads, or the noses and ears. The Bas Mor smiled, deeply proud. Pian had passed the final test. He had enjoyed killing his parents, had taken his time, had listened to them scream. Perhaps one had watched the other die and begged for his or her life. The Bas Mor rubbed his hands together; his body rocked back and forth in perverted joy. "Yes, yes, Pian, my greatest creation, my heir, is truly ready to assume his duties."

chapter 8:

OVERCOMING FEAR

Cean was exhausted, physically and mentally. He walked as in a dream. The sun baked his skin. Sweat rolled down his back. Head down, his sword on his back an unbearable weight, Cean leaned into the hill, struggling to place one foot before the other. His sandals rhythmically slapped the stone path. The road doubled back up the face of Creogh Radahar, but much more steeply than before. In some parts, the road gave way to wide stairs cut into the face of the mountain. The tremendous slope sapped his strength. When he thought he could go no further, he found a small garden cut into a wall on his left. No wider than one of the homes chiseled from the rock face, this sheltered haven held a trickling spring that flowed from the rock face into a pool created by a low stone wall. The masonry of this peaceful enclave was covered in ivy and the perfume of flowers filled the grotto.

Cean lowered his head and trudged toward it. As he drew closer, he heard chuckling, and, looking up, he saw the same old man sitting on the low wall, patting a white stone, inviting Cean to sit down next to him. But as Cean approached, his vision seemed to cloud, then double, and it wasn't the old man sitting there, but it was an old woman with a soft smile on her lined face, with bright, laughing blue eyes and long white hair. Cean staggered and blinked. Cean knew he was a mess, but he didn't think he had hurt his head. His tunic, once white, was blood-stained and hung in tatters around his waist. His upper body was covered in dried blood and sand. Sweat burned as it seeped into cuts and abrasions. He squinted through the light at whatever sat on the low, white wall and then rested his head in his hands, his elbows braced on his widely spread knees. Cean had nothing left to give.

The old woman dipped a piece of cloth into the pool and placed it on the back of Cean's neck. She cleaned his back, gently straightened him up, and washed his face and chest. Cean never opened his eyes. She dripped more water over his head, but he never felt it; he began to slip from the wall and ended up sitting on the flagstones, his back against the wall, his head hanging down. Cean Mak-Scaire was sound asleep.

An old man stood watch over Cean's defenseless body. He remembered other boys who had come before—a long line of innocents chosen without their consent, each with a special ability and personality. He remembered the victories and defeats—so many deaths. *What special creations these men are,* he thought. *So small, so limited in vision, so short-lived, yet some of them are so determined to become more and better than they are. They love so deeply and fight so fiercely. They are noble beyond belief, but their feet are often made of clay. And now this boy, no longer a boy really, but not yet a man, who might carry the hopes of mankind into the future.* Cean slept peacefully at the old man's feet, his head resting against the man's knee. The old man gently put his hand on Cean's head, like a father does to a son he loves, a father unable to tell that son what he knows and what he feels, what he dreams of and what he fears. A father who hopes, somehow, that those things might pass into the child's heart and soul, before his son leaves, before he stops listening.

Cean had to continue. Keeping his hand on Cean's head, the old man closed his eyes, murmured a few words, and vanished. Cean woke up and felt wonderful. He knew he had had beautiful dreams but couldn't remember them. Regaining his footing, he noticed that the old woman was gone. His body no longer hurt, and he found a large clay cup filled with milk next to a fresh loaf of bread and a small tub of butter. "Thank you," he said, hoping he would be heard. Cean tore off a piece of bread, said the small prayer that he'd learned from his mother, and dragged the bread through the butter. He ate for the first time that day. *I guess I'm not alone after all*, he thought. As he ate, Cean looked across the street and saw that the shadows had climbed higher on the eastern walls, but not by much. His nap, however refreshing, had been short.

He finished his meal and wiped his hands on the remains of his tunic, something his mother had always scolded him for. He looked around his shelter once more and resumed his trek up the hill. Cean wondered how many more men would stand against him. He knew he was being reworked, like a piece of molten bronze under a skilled blacksmith's hammer, but who would he be at the end of the day, if he made it that long?

After a long while, he reached a section of road that gave way to a staircase running vertically up the mountain. Cean couldn't see the top of the staircase because it followed the curve of the mountain face. So, he didn't know how high he would climb. There were no railings or walls on either side of the stairs. He decided that he would stay in the middle and keep his eyes glued to the stones in front of him.

Cean climbed, and he felt the wind that he had not felt in the superheated valley called the Path of Endurance. The wind pushed on his left side, making him adjust and readjust his weight to keep his balance. He continued to climb higher; he thought about how high he was, and he moved slower. His legs shook, and his arms became weak. He knew he couldn't look up to see how far he had to go, because he would lose his balance. His eyes stared straight ahead. The sword harness cut into his shoulder and banged his back as he climbed. In midstep, a large bird, maybe a hawk, screeched to his left and exploded out of a crevice in the rock face. Cean jerked his head in that direction. He saw a shape and an explosion of feathers and found himself staring directly into the sun. He began to lose his balance, regained it, but froze as he looked out at the castle. He had made the deadly mistake of looking down, and he had the impression that he was standing on the edge of the world, about to step into empty space. In fact, he *wanted* to step into the air; he had a tremendous urge to leap to his death. It would be so easy just to let go and fall. The wind was in his face as he struggled to keep his balance. Cean was terrified. He panicked. His body swayed; he was losing his equilibrium. He closed his eyes and tried not to scream. No one would hear him; no one would help. He tried to get a hand on a step to his right but couldn't find his grip as his body swayed to the left, moving him closer to death. Again, he felt the pull to let go and heard a voice saying, *Do it. Do it.*

His whole body shook in fear when a second voice said, *Turn right, Cean. Do it now. Don't surrender.* The voice calmed him. He knew he was not alone. He would not give in. Gingerly, he shuffled his feet, unable to lift them off the stone, and turned toward the face of the mountain once more.

Cean leaned forward, placing both hands on a step even with his chest. He was severely shaken. He took breathed deeply and gathered himself, waiting for strength to return to his legs. When he was ready, he began his ascent once more, thinking about the voice in his head. For the first time in his life, Cean felt he had someone, or something, watching over him other than his mother and father. Could the old man have been telling him the truth? Were the marks on his arms that special? And who could do something like this? Cean climbed slowly but steadily. He passed the curve that had blocked his vision earlier, and he could see the top few stairs above him.

Conquered by his fear, Cean completed the climb and fell to his knees. After a few moments of rest, he straightened up and looked around to find a path. Instead, he saw another plaza cut into the mountain. The plaza was lined with men on three sides, the fourth being open to him. Each man stood with his hands clasped behind his back. Each wore a simple white tunic, and none wore shoes. The interior of the plaza was covered with grass, and the area was perfectly level. In the middle of the grassy area stood a man with his feet shoulder-width apart, his arms hanging loosely by his sides. He, too, was barefoot. As Cean approached, he saw that this warrior was slightly smaller than him. His body was lean and hard, the muscles long and strong. His skin was covered in drawings that Cean knew had been carved into his skin with knives and colored with ink. The man wore a gray robe and gray pants. A red sash held a tunic closed around his waist. As Cean watched, the man removed the tunic and tightened the sash. He had very short dark hair and black eyes. Cean initially thought they were about the same age, but as he got closer, he realized the man was probably ten to twenty years older than him.

Cean tried to walk around the man, who blocked his way. Cean looked at the lines of silent men frozen in the sun. Cean tried to go other way, but the man blocked him again. Cean stepped back and looked into his opponent's eyes. They were empty and black. Cean had seen plenty of shark eyes like that. He hated the flat, black, remorseless stare.

Cean drew his sword. Twenty men left their stations and surrounded him. They were ready to fight, and Cean got the message. He stuck his weapon into the ground, took off his harness, and removed his sheath and knife. He put all of it to the side and resumed his position before his opponent. The silent men moved away. "My name is Cean Mak-..." He never got to finish. The soldier leapt into the air after two incredibly fast steps and, covering the distance in a flash, kicked Cean in the chest. Cean flew back, landing flat on his back, unable to breathe and in severe pain. While he was not trained in hand-to-hand combat, Cean knew enough to move as fast as he could. He rolled to the right and continued to roll as his enemy tried to crush his skull with a series of heel stomps. Cean needed space to recover. In mid-roll, he reversed directions. He caught his opponent with one leg on the ground and one raised to deliver another blow. Cean rolled through the planted leg, knocking his foe down. Cean sprang to his feet. His opponent was already standing, ready to launch another attack. Cean mirrored his stance. He tried again. "I am Cean Mak-Scaire. I have been summoned by Kon-r Sighur. Who stands in my way?"

"Dana Fear stands before you. Fight." Those were the last words either man spoke. The sun moved across the western sky. Fear was a master of his craft. Cean's body began to glow with large red welts, evidence of Fear's mastery. Soon, blood ran down his chin and chest. Both eyes were swelling. Cean had landed his own blows, but Fear looked as fresh as when the fight began. Cean's speed saved him from early destruction, yet Fear was not much slower, and he was skilled.

They circled one another, looking for openings. Cean had learned much, but he was hurt. His ribs had taken a beating; breathing became difficult. Fear began to focus on Cean's damaged ribs. Fear would feint to Cean's head, and when Cean raised his hands, Fear would land a powerful kick to the ribs. Cean felt the end drawing near. He was learning to fight, but not fast enough.

Fear drove another kick into Cean's side. Cean took the kick, gasped in pain, pinned Fear's leg to his side, and threw a lightening rigid finger strike at Fear's eyes. Fear raised his arms to block the strike. He saw the trap too late. Cean snapped out a straight kick into Fear's solar plexus. He put his soul and what was left of his body into the kick. Fear couldn't move fast enough. The hard ball of Cean's foot sunk into Fear's chest, hitting a complex, fragile nerve center. Fear staggered backward, but didn't fall, a feat that amazed Cean. Fear was frozen in place, unable to move, unable to breathe, his body stiff and beyond his control. Cean moved in and landed a thunderous blow between Fear's eyes. They had brutalized each other for more than an hour, and he didn't want to continue. Fear went down hard, and Cean was right on top of him, fist raised, waiting for him to move. He didn't. Cean waited, ready to strike. Fear was out cold. Cean stepped away and fell on his back in the grass. He felt like he was going to die. His entire body hurt. He could barely breathe. His eyelids were heavy.

A grating voice brought him back to his senses. "You should have killed me, boy." Cean heard the voice from miles away. He struggled to stand, trying to shake the cobwebs from his head, getting ready to fight. Standing, he saw that Fear was still on the ground. He was trying to get up, but he couldn't. Cean had damaged something in the man.

Cean knelt next to him. "I never wanted to fight you."

Fear looked into Cean's eyes with those dead black pools of nothing. "You had no choice. I was your last challenge. Stripped of all weapons, will he stand and fight? Can he take the pain? Will he submit? Will he run? What have you learned, boy?" A soldier brought a stone jug of water, bowed, and handed it to Cean, who, instead of drinking, held it to Fear's lips.

He thought about the question. What had he learned? After a moment, he said, "I can fight with or without weapons, but I do not enjoy it. Fighting is not a game. I can kill people and be killed. I can be injured. I feel fear. I panic. I am human, like you, like everyone, and yet, I am not like everyone. I am different." He thought again, looking into Fear's dead eyes. He decided he would not mention the old man. "I might be one of you, but you all want to kill me. You see me as a threat, but I'm not; I know it. I have been tested and still live. I need to go on. I need to find the answers that Kon-r can give me. I must go."

Cean stood over Fear. He bent and offered him a hand. After a moment, Fear gripped Cean's hand to pull himself up. The two stood close. Neither broke eye contact. Each was ready to fight again. Two of the deadliest men on earth were making up their minds about one another. After what seemed like an eternity, Dana Fear stepped back and bowed slightly. Cean let out a breath and bowed lower. Raising his head, he saw that the cohort of men along the edge of the grass had fallen to their knees, forehead and palms pressed into the green grass. Cean whispered, "Thank you, Fear," and took up his weapons and began to walk away. Fear's men, now standing, bowed as their master had and moved aside for Cean Mak-Scaire, who resumed his path with head held high and tears in his eyes.

ċhápteɹ 9:

Red Lesson

The Bas Croi sat on a black basalt throne. *So much for memories of home*, he thought. He craved more knowledge about the high priesthood. The Bas Mor had told him that he would develop powers, depending on his strength, and that he might be able to travel back in time through the memories of the lineage of high priests. But no priest had ever been strong enough to get back to the beginning. The Bas Croi was determined to be the first. There were so many questions about the struggle and the figure of the Warrior. And who were those who fell in flames every night?

The Bas Mor made it crystal clear: The Warrior was the Bas Croi's deadliest enemy. Croi closed his eyes and slowed his breathing. He turned his thoughts inward and directed his consciousness to an image of the Bas Mor. He found himself entering the mind, the energy, that was once the Bas Mor. Croi saw the glee that the Bas Mor had experienced as he had tortured and trained Croi. Croi sensed another mind within Mor's: it was Mor's master. The Bas Croi entered that mind and saw the sickly child that became the Bas Mor. Croi continued to leap from mind to mind, learning the history of the priesthood's struggle. He saw brilliant victories amidst terrible suffering, bloodshed, and disease. He learned subtle strategies that had been put into place. The Bas Croi marveled at the accomplishments of the past and the effect they had on the present. Croi began to understand his pivotal role in history, and he thoroughly understood the hatred of the Council that had made strong priests and their commanders wail in frustration. For every strategy they deployed, the Council had always countered and been victorious.

The Bas Croi strained to focus deeply on the past. Sweat dripped from his contorted face. Each succeeding mind was more difficult to enter. Croi fought on; he was getting closer to the beginning. He had to understand the dreams. He pushed harder; his breath came in gasps as he writhed on his throne. But it was no use. He couldn't force his way through. A black wall of force seemed to threaten his very existence. He thought he had been pushed back to the present, as if a huge door had slammed shut behind him. The Bas Croi sat alone in the dark, exhausted and frustrated. He would try again. He would keep trying. Perhaps his power would grow as more blood flowed.

The Bas Croi opened his eyes and began to breathe once more. He could see clearly in his black crypt, and he became restless. Knowing the past was interesting and necessary, he decided it was better to focus on the future. He had much to do now. First, he had to impress his authority upon his commanders who, he thought, were not his commanders at all. They were the Bas Mor's commanders. As such, the Bas Croi did not trust them. He was not convinced of their loyalty. He decided that he needed to show them his power in order to ensure his men would give him the proper respect and that they would fear him. Next, he had to plan the riots that would divert the Marfach Gardei, while his real attack would infiltrate the tunnels below the citadel. Croi had to find unwitting citizens, thousands of them, whom he could bend to his will. He needed to instill in them his hatred and desire for destruction. He looked forward to using some of those new abilities he was promised.

Also, he had to decide where he and his men, not to mention their equipment and supplies, would go after the fall of Athlan. With great insight, the Bas Mor had taught him the geography of the world and had taught him about the people in that world. The Bas Croi had learned even more as he sifted through the minds of the past high priests. He knew that there were many opportunities across the seas to continue his work, but choosing one was the trick. He could not make a mistake.

First things first, he thought. There were twelve commanders, and he summoned them with a thought. *Come, now.* The Bas Croi waved his right hand, and the room filled with spectral green light. The commanders entered the crypt and stood before the throne. None looked into Croi's eyes—his silent summons had shocked them. They were nervous in his presence. Croi enjoyed their discomfort. These commanders had a long history. In fact, their roles went back to the very beginning of the Great Conflict, just as the role of high priest had. There had always been twelve commanders, and they bore one of twelve names, the significance of which the Bas Croi could not yet determine. He savored the names in his mind: Ture-el, Danii-el, Neqa-el, Azaz-el, Baraq-el, Semy-az, At-az, Akabek, Arist-az, Sith-ast, Gon-tar, and Kasa-ta: his death commandos. Now they would learn who their master was. Now they would relearn the lessons of fear and pain.

"I have summoned you because there is a rumor that one of you is a spy of the Council. I have also heard whispers that one of you does not believe I am the Bas Mor's true successor. I will ask only once: who among you doubts my authority?" The Bas Croi thundered those words that echoed from the green walls. Every commander, save one, dropped to his knees, each loudly proclaiming his innocence and fidelity.

The man known as Baraq-el stood before the Bas Croi, proud and confident in his own strength and deeds. "I will not grovel before you, Croi. You have my respect and loyalty, but I require the same from you. I asked the same from the Bas Mor, and you are no different nor better than he."

By this time, the men on their knees also had their heads pressed to the stone floor. They tried their best to become invisible. With any luck, they would have a chance to leave the room alive. Each one silently thanked Baraq-el for becoming Bas Croi's target. They flinched as the Bas Croi thundered, "Your pride condemns you, Baraq-el. Admit your treachery before your equals, and your death shall be faster than it could be."

Baraq-el couldn't swallow. His mouth was a desert. He would not back down. "I have not betrayed you," he croaked. "I am your best and most loyal commander. The Bas Mor honored me as such many times. That is the truth."

Bas Croi's laugh sounded like the hiss of a snake. "Truth? What do you know of truth? Very well, Baraq-el. If you want the truth, I shall give it to you." The Bas Croi raised his hands and extended his fingers towards the hapless soldier. A pulsing red light emanated from his fingertips, surrounding Baraq-el in a transparent, red cocoon. Once Baraq-el was completely encased, Bas Croi raised his hand, and Baraq-el elevated from the floor. Heat began to build in the crypt, and the prostrate men on the floor dripped sweat. Baraq-el tried to scream, but no sound escaped his terrible red prison.

The Bas Croi closed his fist and the red aura squeezed Baraq-el's suspended body. Croi squeezed tighter. Blood began to spurt from the tortured commander. Baraq-el's eyes flew from their sockets, landing on the floor in front of his shivering comrades. The Bas Croi continued to twist his clenched fist, and bits and pieces of blood and flesh flew, landing on the men below. Blood sprayed across the room, drenching everyone except the Bas Croi. The terrible crack of bones echoed through the bloody chamber of death. Flesh ripped as joints popped. No one dared look up; they vomited on the floor, disgusted by the rain of human flesh. Croi shook his fist once more. What was left of the man once called Baraq-el exploded in a cloud of red gore.

The remaining commanders were covered in human waste. None moved. All whimpered like beaten dogs.

The Bas Croi smiled. The lesson had been nicely taught and, hopefully, well learned. A new commander would be elected from the ranks through a gruesome trial by combat. Croi decided that whoever won the title of Baraq-el would have a number of special, private sessions with him to make sure the new commander understood completely who his master was. Bas Croi waved his hand again, and the green light of insanity was extinguished. The Bas Croi slipped out of the room through a secret door behind the throne, while his surviving commanders squirmed and groveled in a dark cesspool of death.

chapter 10:

FAMILY

Torven Lok stood on the prow of his ship, the *Ban Colm*, "White Dove." He was a massive man with blond hair and dancing blue eyes. Called Tor by most, he had been captain of his ship for more than a decade. Tor had seen most of the known world as a trader, and before that as a captain in the marine division of the Marfach Gardei. After years of fighting, Tor had grown sick of the slaughter. He had lost his focus. He came to believe that the enemies weren't enemies anymore, they were simply people being killed to satisfy the desires of the rich. Tor knew Athlan and Athlanean traders had to be protected; he knew that certain tribes and races had been attacked and defeated because they were, or would be, a deadly threat to Athlanean culture. He knew that many deserved to die, but not the children nor usually the women, and not the poor, dumb peasants who had no choice in the matter.

He recalled the day he resigned—something very few Gardei ever did. Kon-r Sighur himself had met with him. Kon-r asked why and how he could walk away from his duty. Tor said, "I can no longer tell who is right and who is wrong, Kon-r. I have killed innocent people for my men, for you, and for Athlan. I can't and won't do it any longer."

Tor remembered how Kon-r's eyes blazed as if he was staring a hole through Tor. After what seemed an eternity, Kon-r responded, "I see neither deceit nor cowardice in you, Torven Lok. I understand your position. What will you do after you leave?" Tor told him about his plans for a beautiful sea vessel and his desire to trade, to be as free as a bird. Kon-r had remained silent for a moment and then said, "You will do well. On your travels, do you think you could see things from a soldier's point of view as well as a trader's?" Tor answered yes. "Do you think you could occasionally deliver messages for me?" Again, Tor agreed. "Do you think you could give me reports once in a while on what your soldier's eyes see around the world?" Tor said yes again. If this was the price of freedom, it was a reasonable one. "Then work hard, Torven Lok, and prosper. I would fight by your side anywhere. Maybe we shall meet again somewhere down the road." They shook hands and went their separate ways. Tor would never forget that day. Leaving had hurt him more than he thought it would. Being a marine captain of the Marfach Gardei had defined him. Leaving, he was no one; he was alone.

But Tor Lok was never one to sit idle. With his savings, he decided to build a ship. He hired carpenters and shipwrights; he brought in wood that was called *oake* by natives far to the north of Athlan. He rented a small shipyard and began to build. He had planned his ship for years. He could close his eyes and see each board, peg, and rope. He constrructed a triple-masted living machine that was unique in the world. The ship had to be large enough to hold a considerable freight, but it had to be fast and dependable. Fast and dependable got you out of trouble. Fast and dependable kept you and your crew alive. His ship also had to be a fighting ship because not everyone on the high seas was friendly. While he had scruples, Tor would kill, and swifter than most.

Tor was no angel, and the years of trade had dulled his moral sensibilities. He was no longer above running goods in the dark into hidden, Athlanean coves. Taxes were fine for everyone else, but they had never appealed to him. Smuggling was like a game to him, a sea-going battle of wits that added spice to what was often a boring business. Tor enjoyed his new life but missed the friendship and emotional charge of battle. His men had been his family; they fought together, drank together, and died together. Battle had been their business. Trade was his business.

Tor looked up into the cool, blue sky. He felt good. Hands on the rigging, he could feel his ship vibrate as it surged through the gentle ocean waves of the Muirseol Sea. *Ban Colm* had the wind and was making great time using sails alone. What made Tor's ship exceptional was its propulsion system developed in secret with a shipwright. The *Ban Colm* had two enclosed channels that ran the full length of the ship on either side. Water entered the front of each channel and was forced back through the tunnels by a series of cogs and screws. Water left the aft end of the channels far faster than the speed at which it had entered. With sails completely inoperative, the *Ban Colm* could exceed twenty knots. It took very little water entering the funnels to start the multiplying effect. Totally becalmed, *Ban Colm* could prime the mechanical pumps by pulling the ship forward with rowboats. Once the stream of water entered the funnels, the propulsion system went to work. Speed was controlled by monitoring the water let into the funnels. This was accomplished by sliding doors that could be moved in and out of the funnel openings from the deck. The ship could be turned by rudder, or, if the rudder was broken, partially blocking the right channel would make the ship turn to starboard, and the opposite was also true. He was quite proud of his system. Buried beneath the water line, his unique invention gave him unmatched speed and maneuverability in all waters and weather. *Ban Colm* was more than a sleek sailing ship. She was the future of sailing.

Speed and maneuverability were not enough, however, in the world Athlan considered its own. *Ban Colm* had to be a self-reliant fighting ship. Small metal tubes extended from the rear deck and both sides of the prow. These tubes also protruded from the starboard and larboard sides of the ship at twenty-five-foot intervals. At the inboard end of each tube was a crystal that collected and magnified light. The light from the crystals was directed within the tubes, which were lined with precisely cut and polished mirrors, placed and tilted for maximum reflectivity and concentration. Light left the narrow tubes in focused fine lines and could travel for well over a mile. When the beams hit something solid, that object began to heat up. Wood burned and metal became too hot to touch. Tor's advantage was that he could destroy his enemies at a great distance without directly killing anyone, unless they were hit with a beam. He also liked the idea of striking them before they could hurt him. Each crystal-powered weapon held a reserve of power in backup crystals that could be inserted on cloudy days or at night. The power supply was not endless, but it did give Tor long-distance fighting capabilities, day or night.

Wind in his face, Tor led *Ban Colm* carrying a full cargo of food-stuffs which were badly needed on Athlan: wheat, olive oil, and a new, white-kernelled food called *ri* from the far corners of the world. With this load, Tor could become a rich man if he could find a buyer, if he could sell his goods for portable gold, if he could quickly land and offload his invaluable cargo, if he could safely get away from the mayhem, if, if, if.... Tor knew Athlan would soon become a place of the past. He had a hard time believing it. He had experienced the power Athlan wielded in the world; he knew the scope of Athlanean greatness. He anticipated the battles that lay ahead. His crew were all volunteers—almost two hundred willing sailors eagerly working through seas, rough and smooth. They asked for little: food, a small share of the profits, but more fundamentally, they asked for honesty and competence. If he demonstrated his ability to lead, protect, and prosper, they were his. The agreement, never spoken, never written, was as ancient and respected as sailing itself. He was master if he held up his end of the bargain.

Tor turned from the sea and watched his crew work the billowing sails of *Ban Colm*. His sailing master, Muir Ar Seoult, stood at the helm, occasionally issuing commands to the young men, two brothers, who manned the wheel. Torven trusted Muir with his life. Muir, older than almost everyone on board, had wild white hair that streamed behind him in the breeze. Bushy white brows overhung deep brown eyes still as sharp as knives. His hands, clasped behind his back, were gnarled and massive. He could still grip and snap small spars; on many occasions, Torven had seen him grip the wheel in dire weather, working the ship by himself, long muscular legs firmly planted on the oaken deck. The old man commanded respect and received it from everyone on board.

Tor's gaze moved along the deck. There was Rok-Tan, his master-at-arms. Tan had served in the Marfach Gardei. Tor hired him after he had been invalided after losing his left eye fighting pirates along the Afrik coast. Rok-Tan was still young and quite capable of extreme violence. He was also an excellent combat teacher. Tan drilled the members of each watch in hand-to-hand combat, archery, and swordsmanship. Aside from Gardei ships, the *Ban Colm* had the best fighting crew that Tor Lok had ever worked with. He noticed that Rok-Tan was watching KT, the only female member of the crew, hanging over the rail washing out items of clothing.

Smiling, Tor remembered how KT had become part of the crew. Years ago, while he was tied to the main wharf in Cala unloading a cargo of northern *oake* plank, a young girl ran down the main street and out onto the dock, her bare feet slapping the wooden planks. She was dressed in rags. She was skinny with wild red hair. Tor had guessed she was ten, maybe eleven years old. Close behind was an older man, balding, with long, scraggly gray hair greasily plastered to the sides of his head. He was dressed only slightly better and carried a thin switch held high.

The girl dodged right and left in her attempt to avoid capture, but eventually she came to the end of the pier and, realizing she was trapped, turned to face her tormentor. Tor, standing along the rail of *Ban Colm*, studied her face. He was surprised to see no fear. The girl braced her feet, raised her small fists, and awaited the worst. Her eyes narrowed and became slitted lanterns. Tor was drawn to her; she was a fighter. The man, breathing heavily, approached her cautiously, fully aware of the fight to come. She crouched as he shuffled closer. He raised his cane, leaped forward, and brought the cane across her forehead and face, cutting both. She went down on one knee, head bowed, and her blood dripped into the swirling ocean below. Everyone on the dock watched in silence. The man raised his cane again and brought it down across her back. She never felt the lashing; she only heard a scream and splash.

Looking up, she saw a very large man standing over her with the cane in his hand. He was dressed in high leather boots, white cloth pants, and a leather, sleeveless jerkin; he had a red cloth twisted around his head, holding his long, golden hair away from his face. He snapped the cane in two over his knee and threw it at the sputtering man in the water. Tor knelt in front of her, not too close, and said softly, "You are no longer in danger, lass. I would like to help. Will you come onto my ship, and we'll fix your cut, give you something to eat, and maybe some new clothes? Then you can be on your way, if you want. My name is Torven Lok, captain. What's your name?" Looking at her, bleeding and defiant, Lok was reminded of a wounded, cornered mountain cat he once hunted: trapped but never more dangerous. He backed away still kneeling, watched, and waited for her to decide. Gulls wheeled overhead, raucously ignoring the drama below. No one on the pier moved. They were amazed to see Captain Lok on his knees before the young beggar girl. Lok bowed to no man, and challengers to his authority had disappeared from the *Ban Colm* years ago.

She stared at Tor. Calmly, in a firm but quiet voice, she said, "I'm KT. What about him?" Tor looked over his shoulder to where she pointed. The man he had pitched into the ocean had climbed up a pier ladder and stood staring daggers at KT, dripping and mad as a wet hen.

Tor stood and took a step toward him. The old man stepped back hastily, held out his hands, and said in a shaky voice, "Wait right there, captain. She's my daughter, and you have no right, none, to get between me and my own. Now stand aside, and let us be on our way if you know what's good for you."

Lok became pale as fresh milk, and, before he tore the man to pieces, he turned to KT and asked, "Is that true?"

Without missing a beat, she answered, "Yes, it's true, but he already sold my brother years ago, and he wants to sell me, too, but I know what those pigs are going to make me do, and I'll die first." Tor could hear the strength and truth in her words. Almost faster than the eye could see, and certainly faster than the man could comprehend, Tor closed the distance between them and threw one punch, the crunch of which echoed over the water. KT's father collapsed into a senseless heap, and a loud cheer broke out along the side of *Ban Colm*. Tor's crew thumped the rail and stomped the deck.

Lok checked his victim, saw no movement, and looked at his crew and growled, "Back to work, you shiftless vultures." Loud guffaws followed as they returned to their duties, another Torven Lok story born for endless retelling.

Tor, ten years later, watched KT—tall, lithe, tough, and smart. He remembered the little girl who took his hand and said, "Okay, what's for dinner?" He smiled. She had walked onto *Ban Colm* holding Tor's massive hand, as if she had lived there all her life. KT could sail the *Ban Colm* as well as any man aboard after years of Muir's training, and in battle, she always fought next to Rok-Tan, protecting his back, protecting her family. Tor watched his people, so proud of them, and wondered how he was going to save their lives.

chapter 11:

SISTERS

Before the Council of Four existed, when Athlan was a much less civilized place, thousands of years before the Great Laws had been codified and adopted, there existed a loosely organized group of women, mothers mostly, who dedicated themselves to raising children the "right way." The right way included instilling the virtues of compassion, the practice of manners, the path of silent courage, and a dogged belief in good works. These values were ingrained in every child who would accept them. Many did accept their teachings; unfortunately, many didn't. The Sisters, which is what they called themselves, were the unseen guarantors of civilization; they were the underlying force that held the fabric of Athlanean life together. They were everywhere and nowhere because they were invisible to the great and powerful of Athlan. They influenced society at its very root: the children. The Sisters wielded the power of love like a gossamer net thrown over all who came within their soft embrace. Those caught by their power never knew, until later in life, that they had been ensnared; even if they had known, the good would not have tried to escape. But many did escape. Athlanean society was tearing itself apart.

When things were getting bleak, the Sisters came together for their first formal meeting. Secretly, they gathered in the countryside, well outside Cathair, in a glade surrounded by ancient chestnut and beech. The sun illuminated the green earth, and motes of dust flickered through the warm air. Two hundred women gathered in this quiet sanctuary. They sat on the grass; a few stood in the cool shadows forced to the edges by the sibilant crowd. The meeting had been called by one woman, someone who'd been no different from the others until recently. She was a woman who had birthed children and suffered the pains that women do. Her name was Celine, and she commanded the respect that all women who struggle to make the world a better place deserve. Long, graying hair, gathered in the back, framed a strong face. Her once fine features had been roughened by life. Her bright blue, intelligent eyes revealed that she knew of life as all women did, but she also knew much more, and had so much to communicate to her people. She happened to be tall, but her real strength came from her calm aspect and extensive experience.

Celine's husband had been a merchant in the city, neither rich nor poor. He traded in basic foodstuffs and inexpensive wines. He worked hard and had always put food on the table, kept shelter over their heads, and purchased their clothes. Due to the constant fighting, however, the city's food supply had dwindled and prices had risen sharply. It was becoming harder for him to continue as an honest tradesman. A thriving black market for goods had developed, and honest businessmen were being pushed aside. Not the strongest of men, Esmer began to take out his frustrations on Celine and their children. An old story, perhaps, but no less horrible every time it is told. One night, after Esmer had drunk the rest of his cheap wine, he came through the door of their simple home and began smashing their plain wooden tables and chairs. He screamed and cried out in rage, feeling useless and impotent. In his despair, he punched his oldest boy, breaking his nose, splattering blood everywhere. When Celine came to the boy's defense, Esmer grabbed her, his eyes wild, and choked her, his mind gone. He became an enraged animal, and Celine, having no desire to die, managed to grab a kitchen knife. Steeling herself, she rammed the knife between Esmer's ribs. The blade disappeared into his body. Esmer's eyes opened wide in surprise. Blood gushed from his side and mouth. His grip on her throat relaxed, and he sagged to the bloody floor. Celine thought then, as she did now, that just before death, Esmer came back to himself and, realizing that he was going to die, silently thanked her with his eyes.

That Celine's transformation began with killing her husband was an irony not lost on her. Violence, particularly deadly violence, was against everything the Sisters believed in. But the insanity of evil had to be attacked at no matter the price. Esmer reflected the general degeneration of Athlanean society, and he carried the disease into their home. As Celine stood over his body, breathing heavily, bloody knife still clutched tightly in her hand, she thought, *When did I pull this from his body?* She stared at the knife, watching blood run down the red blade. Time stopped, and her vision turned inward. She saw Athlan in a red haze, a haze created by fire and the blood of countless citizens. She saw dead mothers and children; she saw the towers of the Ban Castlean crumbling; she heard the death cries of thousands; and she knew the destruction was not limited to Athlan. She was seeing death throughout the world, and through the red haze, she began to see a face, but it wasn't one face, exactly—it was a composite of many faces, all with mad, red eyes and leering grins.

She screamed and tried to blot out the collective image of hate but could not. It seemed to get closer to her, and as it did, she could hear it talk—it was talking to her. How could it talk to her? Did it know her name? And then: *I see you. I will find you. You are new to the battle, but you will learn quickly, because I will kill you quickly. Oh, yes, I come for you, woman; you are almost mine now, murderer. Ahhhh! Did it feel good? Did you like killing him? Do you want more? I can give more, much more. I will learn your name, woman, and you shall kill for me when I have finished with you. I...*

She dropped the knife and nearly collapsed next to it. What was the evil that crept into her mind? She was in shock. The evil she had confronted was beyond anything she had ever experienced. Celine gagged and wretched the meager contents of her stomach onto the wooden floor. She broke into a cold sweat, and her breath came in labored gasps. Whoever had threatened her was a powerful being dedicated to the death of everything good, including the Sisters.

Celine remembered times in the past when she thought she knew certain things were going to happen, particularly relating to her children, but many women had those feelings. This had been different. Staring into her husband's blood, she had left her everyday existence, left her husband's dead body lying next to her, left her children staring in the doorway, and she gazed out on a world she knew nothing about. She had found pure evil, or evil had found her, but she had closed her mind, ending contact. What did it mean? Could she do it again? She moved, and once she did, she was quick. Celine gathered her children—two boys and two girls. She packed up everything they could carry, and they left their simple home, never to return. Her husband remained uncovered on the floor, spared from the horrors still to come.

Athlan rumbled around the glade, which seemed an oasis of calm. Celine abandoned her reverie and stepped onto the flat top of a tree stump. The soft murmur of the Sisters subsided. Celine studied the expectant gathering, wondering how to start, what to say. How to explain what had happened to her—how to explain what she had become, what they still had to become? A small but wide woman, curly black hair surrounding a wide face of creases and smiles, called out, "Talk, Celine! We haven't made our way here to act as if we are all waiting for our husbands to say something meaningful to us!"

The women laughed, and Celine suddenly felt better; she felt the old bond of common experience. "Thank you, Helene, for reminding me who we are and what I am. Women of Athlan, Sisters of life! I called this formal meeting, the first of its kind, to tell you of developments never before witnessed in our country." She heard low whispering in the glade. She had their attention. "For hundreds of generations we have striven to make our sons and daughters good people: nothing more and nothing less. We have adhered to an unwritten code: good has to be nurtured; if goodness grows in your garden, evil will not." She looked out over the crowd. *So far, so good.* "When we have been successful, we have instilled the virtues of charity, courage, and hard work with the goal of improving our family, then our country." *First hurdle cleared.* "Unlike many others, we have never based our beliefs on the existence of supernatural powers who judge our actions and who will reward or punish us based upon those actions. These thoughts we have left to philosophers and priests. We have always believed life can be good, but we need to make it so. If left untended, our fields become choked with thorns. If left uninstructed, our children become thorns that cut us to shreds. We have dedicated our service to the practical matter of raising our children to become men and women of good character, capable of leading others to a better life. Long have we believed, and long have we fought the battle." She waited. They watched. *No objections. No questions. Good.*

"I don't have to tell you what is happening around us. You can see it as well as I can. Our lives in Athlan are coming to an end. The island is crumbling, as is the society we have nurtured for many years. The center cannot hold, and we are cast adrift. Does anyone here see things differently?" Again, no one answered. There was no sound other than the muffled noises of a dying island.

But the Sisters were not comfortable. Celine could see the apprehension on their faces. They were being led somewhere, and many were unsure they wanted to go there, wherever "there" was. "We are here to discuss a few things: do we go live somewhere else if we can, or do we die with our families and our island?" That got them. "Secondly, I offer each one of you a chance to be more than human, a chance to fight unthinkable evil with the unfortunate certainty of losing all that you have, including your families. Which of you wants to share the pain of this drastic course with me?" And, with that question, the once-silent glade became a maelstrom of stamping feet, shaking fists, and questions shrieked in anger and fear.

CHAPTER 12:

PATH OF STONE

Cean walked away from Fear victorious but exhausted. His clothes were in tatters, and his body was a collection of bruises and cuts. He was in a daze and had no idea where he was going. Leaving the battle square, wiping tears and sweat from his eyes, he looked ahead and saw an ornate gate cut into the mountain rock. He squinted against the light, trying to see above the doorway. There was nothing but mountain above the lintel. No windows, no battlements, no towers. Nothing but white stone, the same stone the Ban Castlean was made of. He lowered his head, almost blinded by the glare, and he staggered against the right pillar of the doorway—a stone sentry who had been standing at attention forever, as far as anyone knew. The silent sentinel's right hand was set firmly on his sword pommel. His left arm held a triangular shield emblazoned with the fist and palm. His determined visage gazed into eternity. Cean's eyes snapped wide in recognition. Checking his own branded forearms, he felt strongly drawn to the ancient warrior, and he knew that they were part of the same story. He looked left and saw an identical guard there. Checking that guard's shield, he found the same design. His breathing was almost under control, and his brain was no longer embroiled in combat. Cean stood still in the bright sun, head down, eyes closed. He was spent, useless as the stone sentinels.

Cean squinted and looked through the door. He could see nothing. His eyes, still operating in the bright sunlight of the battle square, failed him. He wanted no more surprises, no more challenges, especially in the dark. His vision could not adjust to the deep shadow on the other side of the gate. He was literally blind to what was before him. *But shadow could be a good thing, too,* he thought. Shadow meant cool, and cool was what his body craved. Besides, he was sure his path ran through this dark gate and that his trial was not over. Still, there was something intimidating about crossing that austere threshold. He felt something on the other side of the door, something... He couldn't put his finger on it. Forcing himself to stand upright, he moved one quivering foot in front of the other and slowly walked through the shadows, arms out in front of him to ward off unseen obstacles. Sand stuck to his feet, scratching the cool stone floor. The sound echoed down the dark corridor.

After fifty paces, including two severe turns that completely shut out the light of the entrance, his eyes adjusted to the darkness. Cean sensed shapes on either side of the solid, cool stone path. Figures seemed to emerge from the walls, and they were much larger than him. As his eyes adjusted, he began to make out some of the details: soldiers in sculpted armor of enormous scale, each figure with its head tilted down toward the path, toward him, as if they were watching his progress. They seemed ready to leap from the walls, swords in hands—to punish him if he faltered. Cean couldn't make out the eyes of the stone giants, but he wasn't sure that he wanted to. His fingers brushed along the wall as he moved, feeling some script chiseled into the surface under each carved image. Were they names of past kings, or famous warriors who had died in the service of Athlan? He couldn't tell. He couldn't see any light source, although light must have been emitting from somewhere, otherwise he would be completely blind. He dismissed both thoughts. He was too tired to think.

His body told him he needed water and rest. Food would be good. He wanted time to think. Leaning his head against the stone wall, gashed forehead soaking up the inky coolness, he thought about the changes in his life. He had a past that he understood. He had a family, and until the day the cursed marks appeared on his forearms, he understood the violent and dangerous present of Athlan. Sitting in the dark, surrounded by menacing stone giants and a shadow history he neither knew nor understood, Cean was ignorant of his new self. He knew he could fight and kill the best warriors, the Marfach Gardei, which meant he could stand and fight anyone. He knew that killing was sometimes a choice; and, although he took no joy in causing the death of another, he felt certain that he would do it again, when necessary.

Still leaning against the cool stone, Cean felt himself relax. His breathing slowed; his shoulders released, and he sagged toward the ground. His arms and hands hung loosely at his sides. For the first time he noticed the deathly stillness of the passageway. Was it a tomb? There was no sound other than his own breath, his own mass leaning against the stone. He stood, listening for what seemed like an eternity, wondering who or what would come to take his life this time. And then a sound in the distance, slow, rhythmic—*plink....plink.....plink*— and he smiled. It was water, it had to be, and it was up ahead.

Pushing off the wall, he walked toward the sound, left hand out in front, right fingertips brushing the wall, head slightly bent forward, as if to protect his face and eyes from an unforeseen threat. He was still very aware of the brooding figures monitoring his progress. Cean stopped. He felt for his sword and knife; they were still there. He wrapped what was left of his clothing tighter around his battered body.

He had not gone far when he sensed something ahead. This was a new ability, although he couldn't tell how far ahead or what it was. He moved slower, the front of his body facing the right wall, left foot forward, right foot back. He bent his knees and kept his back straight and head up, then pulled out his knife and held it in his left hand. He drew his sword in his right, pointed it to the ceiling, ready to slash. He began to shuffle forward, weight centered in his stomach and thighs, as steady and silent as he could: left foot forward, right foot followed, left foot forward, right foot followed, back stiff, head up, eyes straight ahead, scanning every bit of floor and wall space on either side. He tried to sense his way through the dark. His thighs throbbed, and he was damp with sweat, even in the cool shadows. Step. Stop. Listen. Step. Stop. Listen. There. *Water dripping into more water, plink... plink...maddeningly close, but something else, a noise, low, repeating, by all the.... laughter...*

Moving slowly, muscles bunched, ready for action, he wondered if they were laughing at him. Who were they? More Marfach Gardei?

Was it Kon-r Sighur or a new challenger? Cean moved forward. The hallway became lighter, so he could make out the surrounding details. The narrow corridor was broadening into a large hall, completely roofed over with stone. The light intensified. There was no fire that he could see, and no smell of smoke. He saw the statues more clearly. They were warriors, and he admired their weapons of stone, once real and deadly, like these men in their day. He saw writing under and above them, extolling each man's virtues, extending the entire hallway on both sides. He saw that the floor was one solid piece of white mountain stone, brilliantly polished by countless footsteps. There were no joints where the walls met the floor, nor where they met the ceiling.

Moving further along the white path, Cean gasped as he looked up at the ceiling. There was a never-ending series of paintings—or carvings, he couldn't tell—depicting battle scenes. Some showed humans caught in the bloody throes of combat, which he now understood well enough. But others portrayed beings that wielded weapons of fire and ice, beings that flew through crystalline blue skies or dark, red-rimmed clouds. Cean saw gleaming figures in white and menacing black forms that seemed to suck the light from an image. White and black couples were intertwined in death. Some figures were fighting in the clouds, where lightning bolts seared the sky, causing winged beings to plummet into fiery destruction. He couldn't move; his neck arched backward; his eyes were glued to the riveting scenes above. He instinctively recognized the scenes but didn't know why. They called to him. His heart responded; he wanted to fight. Gripping his weapons, eager for battle, he stood oblivious to past or present, craving a glorious future. And that is why he never saw her coming, never knew she stood directly behind him.

chapter 13:

RITUAL

Later, Cean would think about that moment. He would wonder how he knew, absolutely knew, that a woman was standing behind him. She was a shadow in his mind, a deep feeling in his heart, a confusing image in his brain. She was surely a woman, but visions of battle, bright swords of fire, and bloody spears of argent surrounded what he thought of as her face. Groups of people, all in white, lined up in huge, square formations, tremendous power shimmering around them, as if they existed in some invincible, invisible cocoon. They waited, watching him.

His mind was in a whirl. He sensed power, as if a solid wall of force stood behind him, ready to grind him to dust. This strong woman nearby did not register as friendly. In fact, Cean classified her as a deadly threat.

He decided. His left foot slid back, opening his left hip, as his right hand drew his sword and powered his weapon through an arc around and over his head to the spot he anticipated her neck to be. As he whirled and her general shape registered in his brain, Cean adjusted his swing, putting his weight and strength into the attack. It should have been a fatal blow. His sharpened blade should have separated the body from her head. But it didn't. As he turned and cut, his eyes met hers. In that instant, he saw her eyes, which burned with a brilliant, colorless fire. His mind went blank. Having already lost control of his thoughts, Cean's body also gave way.

As he fell, his sword continued its destructive arc, but caused no damage. The last sound he heard was a loud, metallic ring that reverberated down the corridor. He had the impression that the frozen stone sentinels of the past were laughing at his martial incompetence. He hit the floor and rolled onto his back, defenseless.

The warrior guardians of Athlan's past were, in fact, laughing, but their mirth had nothing to do with him. They laughed so hard because Fear and his men, still working outside in the battle square, thought they heard thunder tearing the mountain apart. They watched as a minor avalanche of rocks, stones, and dust slid down the mountainside and piled before the dark gate. Fear walked over to the ancient door.

He alone had the courage to approach. Standing at the entrance, he listened to the unearthly laughter. Goosebumps covered Fear's flesh, and he realized the eyes of both carved sentinels had shifted until each was looking directly at him through orbs of cold stone. He had no doubt that they could see him, and he had no doubt that if he tried to enter the hall, they would stop him. There were tales about the carvings deep in the hall. Fear knew Cean was the reason for the thunderous roar, and he fervently wished the young man well. Fear dropped to his knees, murmured a prayer, stood, and walked back to his spellbound men. He approached the closest Gardei trooper, dropped him to the ground with a compact right cross, and shouted, "Alright, ladies, back to work."

The stone warriors continued to laugh as Cean's body lay sprawled on the stone floor. The woman looked down at the body and smiled. She, too, laughed, and that wonderful sound spurred the warriors of stone to deeper merriment. After a long moment, she looked at each carved knight and stepped over Cean's prostrate body. She had stopped laughing and so had the stone warriors. She tilted her head and studied the battle scenes on the ceiling. The hall and corridor were now very bright. She pulled back a white sleeve from each arm and held out her forearms for each of the heroes to see. Etched into her arms were the fist and palm—the universal signs of battle and peace. They burned with silver fire.

Without apparent effort, the knights leaped from the walls and formed a circle around her and Cean. No longer made of stone, each hero was once again a young warrior at the pinnacle of his power. Each stood, flexing muscles that had not been used for many years. Each champion moved his hand to his sword pommel, instinctively making sure he was still ready to fight. Once the circle was complete, every hero pulled back the sleeves of his own jerkin and chainmail. Their fore-arms bore the same fists and palms as hers, but theirs were not made of fiery lines of silver. Theirs were worn lines that had weathered long, violent lives. Some brands were crisscrossed with scars, while others had pieces missing where the flesh had been cut away in combat. She held their gaze, and as she did, each lowered his arms to his side and nodded, confirming their ancient allegiance. She then pointed down toward Cean's chest. A beam of crystal power shot from her finger and seemed to pierce his heart. His back arched, and he cried out, but he did not regain consciousness. Still unaware, he lay breathing heavily on the floor.

Then each knight drew his sword and placed the tip of his blade around Cean's heart; twelve points of blood welled onto his chest.

Each hero concentrated on his own sword point. Like molten metal in a blacksmith's furnace, each of the blades of became a river of flame, which flowed down into Cean's chest. Anyone watching would have expected Cean to become a charred husk, but he did not. Instead, he writhed on the floor and, arching his back, cried, *"Yes!"* in a voice that filled the hall and corridor as if it was a god's voice. The awful fire in the weapons dissipated; the men sheathed their blades.

All of the old Warriors had been commoners when they were young, and all had been shocked by the appearance of the fist and palm on their arms. They had gone through the same initiation except he who was first, and that man, standing there now, smiled at the newest member of the brotherhood as Cean lay helpless on the floor. His name was Ro-Fannin—first captain—and his smile was bittersweet, as were the smiles of all the Warriors. They knew the life that Cean was doomed to live—the pain that would come from loneliness that could overwhelm a man with no family, no wife, and no love. He would see his friends get killed in combat or slowly taken by old age. They knew the sacrifices Cean would make because they had made them. Here, years after their own glorious service, many of them remembered the pain of their isolation. They were different, chosen, and they had paid for the honor of their heartbreaking magnificence.

Yet this initiation, this gathering, was different. Two Warriors existed at the same time, which had never happened before. They met her eyes, waiting for more. She measured them; although she had their measure years ago. They all knew her as a messenger from a higher power. They took her abilities for granted. These men had come to grips with the existence of forces beyond their understanding. They had seen too much to doubt. The ancient Warriors didn't have all the answers, but no one did, and they accepted that.

She began, "A battle comes, brave ones: an inevitable confrontation of powers. Your past victories and losses have led to this place and time. Change is in the wind, and, as always, blood will be shed. The final victor has not been decided." This last statement shocked the stalwart Warriors. They had always accepted, as a matter of faith, that they would triumph in the end, that a Warrior would be the instrument of final victory. They recovered quickly. These men, now young again, had seen and done things that had opened their minds to the endless possibilities of the universe. The endless battle was as real to them as the weapons they carried. The existence of otherworldly powers of was not a matter of belief for the Warriors; it was a matter of fact. They stood silently, relaxed, experienced, deadly, waiting for the Cath Angeal to reveal their role in the coming slaughter.

chapter 14:

THE FIRST CURADH

The Cath Angeal stepped away from Cean's inert form and walked toward the central hall. The circle of Warriors parted, let her pass, closed up behind her, and followed her. In the center of the hall was a large, circular stone table surrounded by fifteen seats. A few months earlier, there had been fourteen finely chiseled, high-backed chairs evenly spaced around the massive table of highly polished basalt. The chairs accommodated the twelve Warriors, the present one—Kon-r Sighur, and the Cath Angeal. The fifteenth was a recent addition, and the reason was now clear: Cean Mak-Scaire would take a place at the table. The chamber was filled with light. The hall, perfectly circular, was supported by ribs of carved rock that soared in beautiful arcs toward an unseen peak. That peak was so far from the floor that the light below did not penetrate the shadows above. The ribs were spaced evenly along the circumference of the base of the circle, and between each rib was a painting continuing the stories told on the ceiling.

The floor was different. Instead of polished white stone, the surface was composed of hundreds of thousands of pieces of polished, colored stones. Most of them were no larger than the last joint of one's little finger and smooth on all sides. They fit together without mortar. The stones were an assortment of perfect geometric shapes: squares, circles, and others. The colors were astounding, and it could take a while to realize that a stunning work of art existed underfoot. Seen from far above, without the table and chairs, was the story of creation as laid down by an unknown artist a millennium earlier. Filling the center of the floor, there was one colossal being of light and power, who was set against a deep blue universe filled with silver stars and burning, red planets. The being pointed its index finger, almost lazily, at an insignificant human form stretched across a barren, rocky promontory. Fire lanced from that hand.

Around the perimeter of the mosaic, other scenes came to life, depicting the development of man, and the advent of woman. Contrary to many legends that existed in the world, this section attested to the fact that the female form rose from the land itself, independent of man, and was at least an equal partner in the power that was life.

Another panel told the story of evil's existence at the fringes of the universe, as well as the recorded incursions and resulting pain and destruction caused by dark power. Many tales were told on the wonderful floor of glitter and gold, yet few had ever read them. The reason was simple, yet inviolable: they weren't for everyone. The beauty of creation as described in that hall was reserved for those who bore the unique marks of the Warrior. For all others, the floor appeared as an impressive mosaic of pretty colors and cleverly crafted bits of stone and glass—nothing more.

The Cath Angeal stood behind her chair, hands gripping each side, eyes closed. Each Warrior stood behind his seat in the same manner, waiting for her. Patiently. Angeal was far away in time, not remembering, but *being* in the past, watching Ro-Fannin as he was selected as the first Curadh, the first Warrior. He was the son of a simple shepherd, ready to assume his father's duties. She found him working his flock in the highlands along the western coast, high up, sheltered in a grassy hollow. Ro had a merry fire going beneath a rocky ledge and was softly playing his pipes. The animals seemed to be comforted by the sound, and he enjoyed playing for them. He was a gentle lad, always daydreaming of better food and pretty girls, nursing the vague hope of doing something important someday. But his father trusted him with the family fortune, their sheep, because he knew that Ro would stand and fight anyone or anything that threatened their flock.

Young Ro, playing a quiet country tune as dusk approached, looked up toward the mouth of the dale through the flames and saw a shimmering light. He stopped playing, lowered his pipe to the ground, and took up his crooked, wooden staff. He stood and waited, watching what appeared to be a woman with long blond hair. The flock made no sounds of alarm, no distressed bleating, but parted calmly, giving her an open path. As she came closer, he saw the intense light in her eyes, and he feared for his life. She could not be human. She had to be a creature of the night, something he had never believed until this moment. She had come for his blood, or worse, his soul. The dale had become quiet, the only sound the steady crackling of the fire. No matter; he would fight her. He gripped his staff with both hands and pointed the crook at his unnatural foe.

She stopped on the far side of the flame. She was wearing a finely linked, silver mail dress over a flowing white robe. She carried a great sword sheathed on her left hip, which hung from a golden chain acting as a belt. On her right hip, two shining objects hung, silver shapes that seemed to writhe in the firelight. She was taller than he was and beautiful, but Ro felt no attraction to her. She was fire and ice. He had been right; she could not be human. He tensed, ready for action, but in his heart, he knew he was defenseless. Nevertheless, he would do his best. Ro risked a brief glimpse beyond the dale, trying to see if she was alone. She was. The dale was as bright as day. The light came from her, although surely that was not possible. His legs became weak, and he began to sweat. Then she laughed, a wonderful sound, and he fainted.

Ro awoke to find himself propped against the rock wall beneath the ledge. He saw the fire first, which seemed to be much larger than before. Then he saw her. She was kneeling on the same side of the fire. Ro knew he should move away, but he did not, could not. He managed the words, "Who are you?"

She tilted her head slightly and replied, "I am the Cath Angeal. I have come for you, Ro-Fannin."

It was as he thought. He was going to die. Ro looked for his staff and found it in the fire. The top end crook was on one side of the fire and the metal shod bottom was on the other. The shaft had burned to cinders. "You have destroyed my only weapon, but I will not surrender easily. I will fight with my hands."

Again, she tilted her beautiful head and answered, "I know you will, Ro. That is why I have come for you and you alone."

"I don't understand. I'm no one. I'm a shepherd, that's all. Why me?"

"You are chosen because you will not give up. It is your nature, and I need someone with that quality. Someone who will fight when challenged, who will fight even though they know they can't win. Someone who doesn't know how to quit. Let me ask you a question. What do you fight for?" The question surprised him. He never really considered a question like that. Why did he fight so hard? Why would he never give in? Why did he resist this beautiful woman?

Ro's voice rose above the crackle of the fire. "I fight because it is the right thing to do. You have no right to my father's sheep, and you have no right to my life. I will fight because you must be stopped. You will take what is not yours. That is not right. How many times have you taken what is not yours? Is that answer enough, demon?" His voice was like loud thunder echoing off the stone walls of the dale. He stood adamant, as if he was carved from stone. His anger overcame his fear, and a Warrior now faced the Cath Angeal—a boy, a shepherd, willing to become a man.

She smiled. "I have chosen well, Ro-Fannin. You shall be the first of your kind. Perhaps an explanation is in order. Please sit down." He did and she began her story, and long hours later, the two sat face to face in silence, embers hot beside them.

After a while, he asked, "This battle, it has gone on forever?"

"Yes."

"It will continue here, on Athlan?"

"Yes, I think so, Ro."

"You don't know?"

"There are many things I do not know, Ro.

"And I and those after me will fight them. Will we win?"

"Again, I don't know. Does it matter?"

Ro considered the question and saw the answer. "No, it doesn't matter. If what you say is true, and I believe it is, we must fight anyway. That is the answer, isn't it?"

"Yes, Ro. That is all we can do."

Ro thought about all she had asked of him. *No more girls, no wife, no children, no farm, no...... Only the struggle, and, probably a bloody death here or in some faraway land, alone.* What choice did he have? She had picked correctly. He could not walk away. It was not in his nature. But he would not submit; he would agree. "I accept. Can you tell me, at least, who you are?"

Nodding, she said, "I am the Cath Angeal, the Death Angel, and I serve the power that would stand by you in this battle, the power that flows through me and will flow into you. I serve the principle of light that embraces your simple but perfect answer as to why you resist. I will not tell you more. You already know the truth at the heart of everything. My words would only confuse you. Will you accept the life and death we offer?"

Ro answered, "Yes." And his fate was sealed, along with the fate of those who followed.

Ro could have said no. *She* could not have said no to her mission, but he could have. So strange: these humans could say no to the power that moved the universe, yet she, the Cath Angeal, a creature of almost limitless power, could not. Yet they were so necessary. The battle this time would be fought here on this earth, and it would be fought and won, or lost, by this man and his duty-bound descendants.

"It is time, Ro. If you would proceed, stretch out your arms, palms toward the sky."

Ro did as she asked. The Cath Angeal reached into the fire with her left hand and removed one of the silver forms she had carried into the dale. It was a branding iron, something Ro was familiar with. The brand was in the shape of a fist. The ancient form glowed white hot as she brought it close to his left arm.

"This is the mark of the Warrior, Ro, which I now burn into your body and soul." She pressed the burning fist into Ro's arm. The flesh sizzled as the brand sunk deep. Ro gritted his teeth, his jaw muscles popping under his skin. His breathing became shallow and fast. The smell of burned flesh suffused the dale. She removed the molten form. Ro looked down, expecting to see his arm a bloody and blistered mess. Instead, he saw a glowing fist and felt no more pain. He experienced a new, raw power. "Next, the open palm: a symbol of control, acceptance, and peace." She took a second burning iron and pressed it into the inside of his right forearm. More pain. His right arm was marked with the open palm of control and peace. His resolve—always strong and the reason for his selection—increased exponentially. He would accomplish his mission, or die trying.

It was done. He was still Ro-Fannin, young human of Athlan, but no longer was he the shepherd son of his father. He was Ro-Fannin, the first Warrior of this world, the deadly right arm of Cath Angeal. He and his line would be the bane of the Dark Master Dorcada and his evil high priests. Holding his arms in front of him, inspecting the lifelike brands, some of the consequences of his pact dawned on him.

"May I take the sheep down into the village and say goodbye to my family?"

She nodded.

"How long can I stay with them?"

"A fortnight will be alright, Ro, but no longer. We have work to do."

It was his turn to nod, and he said, "Where shall we meet again?"

"Look for me at the dawn of the fourteenth day. Wherever you may be, I will be there also. Spend this time well, Ro. You might never see your loved ones again." The Cath Angeal turned and floated out of the dale. Ro watched and was no longer surprised by her.

Ro-Fannin, first Warrior, threw wood into the fire, leaned back against the stone wall, and planned his route back to his father's village. He would not lose any of the creatures under his care. His would make his father proud.

chapter 15:

You Will Die

The Cath Angeal returned from her reverie. She opened her eyes and studied the table, looking at her "boys," each not much more than a child when they assumed the duties thrust upon them. Each had died in service of her and had asked no questions—had never, in fact, asked for anything "extra," had never complained about his harsh life. Every time one of them had died, the Cath Angeal had felt anguish, a great sense of loss. More painful still was her knowledge that another innocent but determined boy was doomed to travel the same self-sacrificing path as those who had come before him. Despite her power, she wasn't immune to human emotions. Every death had caused her more pain than the previous one.

As these young men were chosen, so had she been "chosen." Like them, she neither questioned nor doubted her greater purpose. Of all the celestial servants—those who existed on a plane between the Great Power of Light and the Council of Four—she alone truly understood humans, because she experienced their pain with the death of every Warrior. She alone grasped the paradox of humanity: the greatness and baseness that resided in each soul and the complicated lives that resulted from this disastrous dichotomy. The Cath Angeal had never been human, but she fully understood their pain.

She began the ritual. The Cath Angeal and her Warriors had no need for vocal communication: their thoughts moved seamlessly from mind to mind. She thought, *Draw*, and each drew his long blade, creating a deadly, sibilant hiss. Each Warrior held his weapon in front of him with both hands, point toward the ceiling, and waited for the next command. *Table.* They circled their chairs and stood before the table. *Place.* Each Warrior placed his sword in a barely visible indentation on the stone table. The swords met in the center. Their weapons were like their owners: solid, dependable, and deadly. Yet now, as the Cath Angeal added her fiery weapon to the circle, her point touching each of theirs, every weapon burned with a fierce, white-hot brilliance.

Well met, Warriors of Athlan. A new Warrior shall be tested and initiated into your ranks, if he passes the final trial. He has done all required of him. The final test remains. In this regard, our meeting here is no dif-

ferent than those that have come before. His life still hangs in the balance.
But there is more that we must discuss. The men leaned forward slightly.
Over the centuries, I have told you bits and pieces of the great cosmic war.
You have been soldiers in that war. While you have slept, the game has
centered here and will come to a conclusion soon.

Ro, as senior Warrior, asked the basic questions. "Why? And what
would you have us do?" Warrior eyes gleamed with passionate antici-
pation.

The Cath Angeal answered Ro aloud with great fondness and
respect. "The world has changed since you fought for its survival, Ro.
There is an ebb and flow to the human condition, a series of moral
and social peaks and valleys. There are times of great insight and ac-
complishment, and there are times of bitter darkness and despair. The
Council of Four that formed around you long ago has disintegrated.
Only the Warrior remains. Three of them fell victim to the decline
of the human spirit. Their deaths have provided an opening for the
descendants of Dark Bas—your old foe, Ro—to grow, organize, and
arm themselves here on Athlan. The battle has been brought to us, and
Athlan is not responding well. The Gardei have retreated behind the
walls of Ban Castlean to avoid killing the rioting citizens they swore
to protect. The strongest force on the planet has its hands tied by its

own oath to protect and serve. Athlan has remained isolated and aloof for too long. There is no help from other peoples of the world. They relish the idea that it is now our turn to suffer. The responsibility for the Great Battle could have been shared, but it won't be. It is our fight and ours alone.

"Why has this happened here?" she asked rhetorically. "The universe was set in motion long ago. Rules were created concerning physical properties, actions and reactions designed to defend against utter chaos. The physical universe cannot break those rules. Worlds were populated, and fewer rules applied to the inhabitants who are free agents capable of independent action. Their future is their own to create—because of this, events unfold over which we have no control. Why has it happened here and now? Chance? Fate? A great plan? Does it matter? When the moment comes, ready or not, each of us must answer the call in our own fashion. I can offer you no more.

"As for your second question, we are required to defend the Right again."

Hesher Dan, the last Warrior to die, asked, "If we die this time, what happens to us? Do we resume our place in the hall? Will there *be* a hall?"

The Cath Angeal answered, "Do you fear a return to the wall?"

"No," was his curt reply.

"I ask simple questions and expect simple answers." The Angeal eyed each Warrior and none flinched from her gaze. They all wanted to know, and in her heart, she felt they deserved to know. "I stand here as your commander and have done so since the First, Ro-Fannin, received the fist and palm. During that time, I have also been your most ardent admirer. Each of you owns a part of my heart. I will sing the song of life and death for you.

"Listen to me, and watch the panels of the ceiling." A column of white light shot from their sword points. The column remained steady, and the shadows disappeared from the far reaches of the arched hall. A beautiful dome hung over their heads, and the panels were blank. "Watch and listen, Warriors." The Cath Angeal sang in a small, sweet voice, and as she did, her words became an endless series of images that moved across the curved face of the dome. The Warriors watched, listened, and wondered.

As scenes of life and death crossed above, her voice rose and fell, gained strength and mellowed, soothed and irritated the senses. The Cath Angeal was not immune to her own power. If the Warriors could have looked away from the drama above, they would have seen her in various forms. She became a Warrior Queen, then a defenseless girl.

Flames took possession of her eyes and her sword morphed into a fire. Wings sprouted from her back. The Cath Angeal became whatever the brutal story demanded, yet always remained the Angel of Death. She battled as a young man; she became an old man. In her voice, the Warriors heard the screams of dying soldiers and animals, the horrified screams of women and children. They listened to the metallic clash of arms and the thunder of an army marching over a withered plain. Some choked on dust, and their throats became parched. Many panted with the combatants.

Some of the action took place in other worlds. Strange beings tried to kill each other under strangely colored skies. Sounds, sizes, and shapes became alien. Winged creatures fought and blood rained down. They saw creatures marked as they were: the fist and palm locations changed as body types changed, but there could be no mistaking the marks or their purpose. The Cath Angeal continued to sing, convincing the Warriors of Athlan to understand the scope of the battle they were engaged in. Eventually, Ro recognized the formation of the Council of Four. He knew those men. In a short while, the images stopped, and the music echoed away. They were alive again, in the present: humbled but renewed. They had been reborn. It was impossible, but the truth was undeniable. What had been a matter of faith became a matter of fact.

The Cath Angeal could see the devotion and passion in their eyes. She owed them nothing less. "Your question was: what will happen to you if you die in the coming battle? Do you still want an answer, Hesher?"

"I no longer require an answer, Angeal. I am content."

"I will tell you anyway. Please sit once more." They did, and she proceeded. "I believe that each of you will die in the coming days. I think Kon-r will die with you. We do not know about the boy lying back there on the floor. When you die, you will not come back to this resting place, nor will you remain part of this earth. You just saw winged warriors dressed in shining white armor as they clashed with other wind riders caparisoned in red or black. The white flyers are my people, and they are called Seraflame in the celestial order. They are spirits that fight on that plane. That is your future."

Ro-Fannin, first of the Warriors, sat with his head bowed. Tears rolled down his cheeks. He spoke clearly. "It is more than a man deserves. I, too, am content."

chapter 16:

TESTED

The Warriors, honor guard or burial party, picked up Cean from the floor. They were gentle, respectful. They carried him back to the Hall. Each man had gone through the next challenge, and each remembered every detail of that trial. Failed Warriors were killed immediately (Ro was the executioner), and then buried in a hidden graveyard on the slope of Creogh Radahar. In Warrior culture, there was no shame attached to failure, only sadness.

The martial escort placed Cean in the center of the circle, on top of the sword points. Each Warrior stood at his position. Their faces were expressionless, their eyes hooded. Cean opened his eyes and took a deep breath. He was lost. "Stand, Cean Mak-Scaire, your time has come." He saw a woman in brilliant battle dress and young men in full armor, arms crossed upon their chests. They surrounded him.

"We will not harm you, fisherman's son. Warriors, sheath your swords." Twelve weapons hissed into scabbards.

Reveal. The knights bared their inner forearms, each marked as Cean was, all his own age. How could this be? How many Warriors were there? Two seemed to cause enough trouble.

"We are here to determine whether a new Warrior will leave this hall alive."

"Who are you?" He was getting angry.

Cath said, "You are to be tested one more time. If you pass, you are a true Warrior. If you fail, you die. Do you understand the terms?"

"Yes. Who will I fight?"

"You will fight yourself, fisherman's son."

"But..."

She cut him off. "Enough. Stand ready, Mak-Scaire, and be true."

She closed her silver eyes, and he was wrapped in a cocoon of white fire. He couldn't move, couldn't see through the flames.

The Angeal stood with him in the fire. "I will administer this test, Cean. I am the Cath Angeal: the Death Angel. I decide who lives or dies. You will be put into situations. You will have to make decisions. Your decisions will have consequences in the real world. If you choose to save people, they will be saved. If you kill, they will die. Your decisions will determine your fate. I can tell you no more. Remember, be true."

Cean thought, *Be true to wha...?*, and he was moving, fast.

"Hold tight, boy. We are there." The Cath Angeal and Cean Mak-Scaire appeared in the small village where Cean grew up. A fountain rushed in the square, and people filled water jugs, talking and laughing as they went about their daily business. The sky was blue and untroubled by the smoke and fumes Cean remembered from his last time there.

"Where are we?"

"You ask the wrong question, Mak-Scaire. You know where we are; you grew up here. The real question is: *when* are we?"

Cean considered her statement. "Are we in the future, when things have become better, or are we in the past, before the troubles began?"

"You are in the past, Cean, before the first major quakes hit Athlan."

He asked, "So my mother and father are still alive?"

"I know you never had a chance to say goodbye, Cean. They were buried in the rubble of your home, weren't they?"

"Yes."

"And you would like to see them again, talk to them, tell them you love them. Yes?"

What game was she playing? "Yes, I'd like to do all of those things and more." Aggressively, he asked in a strong voice, "What do you want of me?"

Good, she thought. *He has calculated the possibilities. He knows he can save his mother and father. The idea has filled his head and heart. He burns to go to them. So, we begin.*

"Cean Mak-Scaire, you have a choice to make. Come with me." They walked across the square into a shaded grotto surrounded on three sides by a bone-white stone wall whose blocks were large and perfectly cut. "Watch the wall. You will see things, and you will decide. Neither move nor talk. Do you understand?"

"Get on with it," he growled.

The surface of the stone wavered, and the white blocks shimmered in rainbow brilliance. Then, as if he were a bird circling high above the earth, he could see his mother and father having breakfast in the kitchen. And then he, too, was sitting at table. They ate and laughed, eyes sparkling as they reveled in each other's company. Cean was mystified. Was this real or an illusion? Cean knew the date of his parents' death. He didn't know the date right now.

"How far away is the Spring Festival?" Cean asked. The elder Mak-Scaire sat back in his chair, staring at Cean. His mother watched him expectantly. Cean held his father's gaze and asked in an authoritative voice, "How long, father?"

The reply was short and sharp. "Ten days." Cean made mental calculations. Their deaths would occur tomorrow morning, the day of the first massive quake. The Angeal had given him precious little time.

"Don't ask me how I know, but we have to pack up everything we can carry and move out onto the plain. We have to go right now."

Ky Mak-Scaire knew his son, and he knew he was serious. He asked one simple question. "Why?"

Cean held his arms over the table, palms up, and said, "Look. Do you recognize these marks?" Maroth and Ky leaned in for a closer look. Their eyes widened as they identified the feared shapes of the fist and palm, the marks of the Warrior. "We have to leave now. I'll answer your questions later. Please, get your things."

Ky pushed away from the table and said, "I've never seen you like this, Cean. But it's clear something is coming, and you know what it is. Maroth, get your stuff. We'll go immediately."

Cean felt like shouting for joy. He began to pack some food into a sack, while his mother and father gathered the things they needed to live for a few days in the open. It was going to happen; he would save his family; he had....

The ground shook violently, knocking all three down. Dust fell from the ceiling, and dishes crashed to the floor. The world turned upside down, and a terrible roar filled their heads. Cean was in a panic. He could barely see his parents. The kitchen was dark, and people in the streets were screaming. *No!* He had been wrong about the day. The end was now. He had time; they were still alive. Cean struggled off the floor and staggered to his parents.

Another shockwave rattled the house, and he fell to one knee, dazed. He could still do it. "Mother, father, get up! Follow me out!" He rose again and moved toward them. Reaching out to his mother, a beam cracked overhead. The ceiling began to collapse. "This is how it happened. This is how they died!" He screamed in frustrated rage, "Noooooo!" And he dove toward his mother's outstretched hand. If he couldn't save them, he would die with them.

chapter 17:

REJECTION

Cean flew, arms outstretched, desperate to reach his mother. He hit the ground hard and skidded across the grass. *What grass?* "No, no! Send me back, I can still save her! No! What are you doing? They're going to die!" Cean jumped to his feet, fists clenched and eyes wild. He found the Cath Angeal standing against the white wall, arms folded across her chest. He charged her. *She must return me*, he thought. He would save them. She raised her hand, palm open, and Cean froze in place. She watched his granite form and saw the pain in his eyes as he strained against her ward. How many more times would she put him through this torture?

He was helpless as his mother and father died, again. Heavy tears coursed down his cheeks, and his heart pounded in his chest. The Angeal moved within inches of him. "Listen to me. They are not dead—

yet. You can still save them. There is time. Do you understand?" She set the barb deeper into his soul. She released her hold on him.

Cean staggered backward and stood, legs apart, fists clenched. "Why did you pull me away? You promised they would live if I decided to save them. You have broken your word. Send me back, witch!"

Calmly, coldly, she said, "I told you the decision was yours to make. Did you think saving or not saving your family was the difficult decision I had in mind? Life is full of choices, Cean. Hard choices must be made. This is no game. Prepare yourself."

Before he could react, Cean was gone from the grotto. He materialized...in the middle of what had been, very recently, a raging battle. He was in full armor, and in his right hand, he held a bloody sword. He carried a shield on his left arm, emblazoned with the fist and palm. A crowned helmet covered his head and the back of his neck. Silver greaves protected his wrists and shins. His body was bathed in sweat, and he stood alone in the middle of a churned-up field and noticed several dead bodies lying in a rough circle at his feet. He drew great drafts of air into his straining lungs. His body began to shake in the aftermath of combat.

Cean removed his helmet and threw it to the ground. What battle was this? He bent down and ripped a piece of tattered cloak from one of the bodies, then stood and wiped the sweat, grime, and blood from his face. A squad of Marfach Gardei approached. They marched in square, a defensive position. *How do I know that?* The square came to a halt. Spear hafts were grounded in a unified *thump*. Cean appreciated the precision and wondered why. He inspected the men and saw that their tunics were torn and blood-stained. Shields were dented and hacked.

A young officer approached Cean. His mailed fist crashed onto his armored chest. He slammed to attention and barked, "Sir, let me be the first to offer my congratulations on your victory."

"What's your name, soldier?"

"Jax, sir. First Officer of Lion Company, first Gardei Battalion."

"I must have taken a blow to the head, Jax. Where have the surviving scum gone?"

"After you killed Amram II, their general, their army broke and retreated into those hills beyond the stream. I came to escort you back to our lines."

"Why the escort, Jax?"

"These dogs have retreated, but scattered units of cavalry are hidden in those folds of earth to the north. This way, if you will, sir." Cean picked up his helmet and slipped it over his head after sheathing his sword.

He turned on his heel, took one step toward the company of Gardei, blinked out of that "when" and jumped into a far worse reality. He knelt atop a large, flat boulder. He was exhausted. An arrow, its shaft snapped off, jutted from the right side of his chest. He remembered discarding his heavy armor so he could breathe. His people, and the remaining Gardei troops, were slowly filing across the Founder's Bridge that crossed the Cold Rush River. Once across, they would have a short march to the ships anchored in Starlight Cove. He had lost many men. Jax was dead. He had watched him fall. This was Cean's last chance to preserve what remained of the army and save thousands from the ravaging horde that was once the disciplined army of the Bas Cor, a high priest of Graxas from the past.

Unlike before, he knew these facts. He was aware of his present situation. Cean raised his head to check on the progress of his people. He nodded in tired satisfaction. *Good.* This was the last of the civilians, and the rear Gardei he had posted at the bridge head would be crossing soon. Then he would destroy the bridge. His engineers had already chopped through the lesser wooden supports and suspension ropes at the far end. People waved to him as they passed, taking strength from his presence. Trumpets sounded. Cean snapped his head toward the vacated battleground and shouted "Stop!" There was a group of children, pushed and contained by a small number of women, who were running as fast as they could toward the bridge. Chasing them was a large cavalry Bas Cor unit on horseback; they all raised long, curved blades. Cean could hear the thunder of the horses, the brutal screams of Bas Cor men. The women and children were silent. Their deaths were imminent.

Cean assessed positions, speed, and angles. Would they make it to the bridge in time? He thought it too close to call. "Sergeant Axt!"

"Sir!"

"Grab every man you can, and follow me across the bridge. Now!" Cean jumped from the rock and ran toward the bridge. He saw Axt forming Gardei. They would be on the bridge in a few moments. Cean yelled, "Faster, Sergeant!" Cean turned and dashed across the bridge. He stopped halfway. The children were flagging, and the women were carrying two at a time as they pushed ahead as fast as they could. They were almost finished. He waved his hands in the air. They saw him, and, taking heart, picked up their speed. By this time, Axt had caught up to him. "Sergeant, this will be close. Fan your men out in three ranks. Let the women and children through, then close up and retreat.

Stay tightly formed. Do not let those horsemen through. Do you understand?"

"Yes, sir."

"Repeat your orders."

"Three ranks, spears out, let them though, stop the horse soldiers."

"Exactly. Get to it."

A woman screamed in terror. One horseman had sped in front of the others. His saber was raised high, and he was close to the last woman who was running behind two straggling children. She would not leave them. She pushed the two young boys forward and turned, weaponless, to face the charging killer. Cean ran faster than ever. He knew the horse and rider would get to her before he could. All three would die. He carried three short spears on his back; he grabbed one. And without breaking stride, arm cocked, he found himself flying through the cold and dark once again.

He screamed in utter frustration. They would all die without him: all of them, women and children. *This is not right, not fair...* he landed in the quiet grotto and moved his arm to complete his throw, but his hand was empty. No spear was launched to save the day. Cean's howl was inhuman. Again, he tried to reach the Angeal with outstretched, murderous hands, and again he froze—impotent, raging against injustice and waste.

The moment of truth arrived. She gave no leeway in this matter. She asked him to make his choice. Who would he save: his parents, or the women and children he didn't even know? Would she have a new Warrior, or would they be burying another unsuccessful candidate? The Cath Angeal waved her hand before his eyes. Cean was released from her hold and was surrounded by a cage of shimmering, impenetrable force.

He screamed, "Release me!" His anguish was palpable. After a moment, he sank to his knees, head down, and sobbed. Defeated.

"Raise your head. Are you so easily deterred? The time has come. You have the chance to save your mother and father, as I have promised, or you can save those women and children who are sure to die if you abandon them. Make your choice, Cean. Who will live and who will die?"

Mak-Scaire was speechless. A simple but impossible choice. How could he let his parents die? How could he let those innocent children and valiant women be slaughtered? Neither answer was acceptable. They all deserved to live, and he could save them all.

No. He was told to pick one or the other. Some would live and some must die. That was what she said. Those were her rules. Cean tried to think rationally. Two lives against many. Selfish love against generous mercy. But they were his only family. Without them, he was alone. The answer was clear, he would save...No. No. That wasn't the answer. No. It couldn't be. He struggled for clarity. He was desperate, but a clever solution would not present itself.

He became angry, and an answer exploded from his lips. "Witch, I will not play your game of death. I will save all or none. I don't hold the power of choice here. You do. You move me like a puppet. You pull the strings and tell me that I am responsible for life or death. NO! I could have saved them all. You are killing them. I reject the choice you have given me. Allow me to save them, all of them, or end this stupid game with my death. I fight for life; I am the Warrior. I do not compromise with evil or death. I reject the terms of your test, and if death is what you offer, I reject you."

CHAPTER 18:

BELL OF NOTICE

Wind whistled off the Western Ocean, raking the crest of Rada-har. The sky was blue and cloudless. A blazing white-hot sun baked the mountaintop. This was the site of the fabled Table of Law. The table, along with four massive chairs carved of black basalt, baked in the punishing heat.

Kon-r sat still in his large black throne, soaking up the heat, a human lizard. Eyes closed, breath shallow, he reveled in the hot wind grazing over his skin. He wore his simple white tunic, revealing his legs and arms to the sun. His sword rested on the table in front of him. He knew Cean was undergoing the test of pain. He had come to the mountaintop to clear his mind, hoping for answers to the deadly problems that defined Athlan. As the last survivor of the Council, the people looked to him for direction and aid. He did not, however, have the patience to deal with a panicked citizenry. They could no longer think straight, nor would they obey instructions. He was made to fight, not pander; to endure, not administer.

Sweat ran down his face. His tunic was soaked. The deeply impressed marks of his office grew hot on his arms, as if they took on a life force of their own. There were rumors of armed gangs roving the countryside. He had sent out scouts to get the facts, but they had not returned. Their deaths were painful but not conclusive proof. He then sent out heavily armed squads of Gardei with orders to gather information using stealth, not violence. These troops returned, but their reports were always negative. They never made contact. In his heart, he feared this enemy, feared the unknown plan, particularly at night. As the Warrior, he could sense certain things others could not. His soul was attuned to the creatures of Darkness. In his heart, he could feel the shadow; in his mind he could see the dark cloud. Death was coming,

Kon-r opened his eyes and looked out to sea. Far below, heavy surf crashed ashore. He could faintly hear the boom as inexorable waves crashed against indomitable stone. There was so much they didn't know about the world and its people. The Gardei had long operated on one principle: it was better to fight enemies on their soil, rather than on Athlanean soil. These victories abroad garnered two results:

the conquered would lose their wealth to Athlan merchants and bankers, and those who survived developed a deep, lasting hate of Athlan, a hatred passed from generation to generation.

Kon-r felt sure he would have to pay for Athlan's arrogance. In the dangerous here and now, many questions had to be answered, decisions had to be made. He felt like a knotted rope was tightening around his skull. Too many ifs, not enough facts, not enough time. Where to start?

His first decision was made. If these shadow forces were coming, if there was to be a fight, he would manage the battle and, at the same time, call for a massive evacuation. He would have to fight a running, rear-guard retreat to the ships. Their escape was, like many battles, about time, space, and concentrated force. And in the rear guard, there would have to be a smaller group of men ready to sacrifice their lives so the rest could make it onto the ships. He would personally select these men and take responsibility for their deaths. He would fight and die with them to the end. This was his duty.

Contemplating his own death, Kon-r's mind calmed. The problems of survival still waited to be solved, but he had centered himself, selecting his fate. He noticed that the wind and waves had stopped, the sea birds froze mid-flight. Kon-r grabbed his blade and waited. He was tense, a fighter awaiting battle. He balanced his weight, ready. No one attacked, but the sound of a gigantic bell filled his head. It rang again and again, driving him to his knees. Then, stillness. The heat returned twofold.

Kon-r pushed himself up from the bare rock, brushed off his tunic, and picked up his weapon. Once more looking out over the island, his vision was blocked by a beautiful woman clothed in brilliant white. Her eyes burned blue fire, and her golden hair streamed out with the ocean breeze. She hovered above the ground, just enough to make her point, as her wings wafted lazily in the breeze. Kon-r, registering initial shock by her apparition, grinned. He knew the Cath Angeal intimately in many of her forms. He had passed her tests. She had counseled him in battle, taught him about the world, about the universe—as much as he could handle. She was the Celestial Battle Queen, and he was her Paladin. He understood the bell. So dramatic. The bell announced the completion of Cean Mak-Scaire's test.

"I am honored, Battle Mistress. To what do I owe this visit?" The Cath Angeal lowered herself onto the rock of Radahar. She would play along with one of her favorite Warriors.

"Have you no idea why I am here, Kon-r? Did you not hear the Bell of Notice?"

"I'm sorry, Celestial Wonder, but, no, I neither heard nor trembled. I was sunning myself, thinking about the fine women I have never met during my travels in your service." He bowed his head, so she would not see the laughter he was desperately trying to control.

She smiled a small, sad smile. *Oh, Kon-r,* she thought. *I come before you in power and glory, and all you have to say is that you are thinking about the cheap strumpets found in every port city this wretched planet has to offer? Oh, how you have fallen, mighty Warrior. Think deeper.*

Kon-r didn't have to think any deeper. "I know why you are here, Angeal. You are the Death Angel. I see the end, and I accept whatever comes for me, but what of the young Warrior? What is his fate?"

"You are summoned to the Temple once more. We must bring this test to an end." Kon-r's heart broke for the boy. The test should have been over by now.

сḣȧртєṛ 19:

CHANGE

The Cath Angeal sped Kon-r through the mountain rock. His mind spun crazily as he crashed back into the reality of Warriors' Hall. He stumbled and caught himself on the massive stone table. He stood in his designated place. Above the table floated the body of Cean Mak-Scaire. He was held in stasis by a column of blue light. His armor was battered and blood-stained. There was a cut across his forehead. A broken shaft protruded from his chest. He was pale. Kon-r studied the past Warriors. They stared straight ahead. No one moved or spoke. The Cath Angeal stood at her place, wearing a simple black robe with a thin, bone-white sash. A black hood covered her golden hair. The fire in her eyes had dimmed. She was as cold and pale as Mak-Scaire's rigid body.

She said, "This boy has been tested, as you were tested. Each of you was given a choice. You made that choice, and now you stand at this table in judgment. As in the past, I will have the final word, but I respect your deeds and sacrifices and would hear your verdict."

Ro-Fannin, the First, spoke. "How was he tested, Angeal?"

"Mak-Scaire's choice was this: he could save his parents from the death they already suffered, or he could save a large group of children and their wards from the cavalry of the Bas Cor."

"Which did he choose?" asked Ro.

"Not so fast, my First. Each of you shall give his opinion on which group Mak-Scaire should have saved. Answer first, Ro."

The First considered for a moment and said the obvious. "They aren't my folks, Angeal. My interests would not be his. I believe he should have saved the children and their wards. His mother and father had already enjoyed many years of life." Of course that would be his choice. It was the right choice. A Warrior had to weigh the good of the many against the loss of a few. A Warrior had to sacrifice everything for duty. As terrible as Cean's choice was, it should have been crystal clear to him. And it was not. She went around the table, looking into the eyes of each man, and every one of them agreed with the First.

Except Kon-r Sighur. "I believe my brothers see this clearly, and their answers come from the heart and are correct. But you have not told us anything, Angeal: times change. Situations change. Are we not in the strangest time Athlan has ever witnessed? How can there be two Warriors at the same time? Why should there be two? Answer me: did Cean choose his parents and abandon the children?"

The Angeal cocked her head as she locked eyes with Kon-r. "No, he did not."

"Did he choose to walk away from his parents, leaving them to die?"

"No, he did not." This last statement, made at just above a whisper, was puzzling.

The Warriors knew that not making a choice was the same as making the wrong one. In battle, decisiveness was a must, even if the choice was to run away. Both options led to death. Kon-r saw beyond the confusion and glimpsed something wonderful. He became excited. "He did something unexpected, didn't he? Something new, something that destroyed the test. What did he do, Angeal? What is holding your hand?" Perhaps Kon-r, Warrior of the Change, was the only one who could have thought the situation through. The others were bound to their time and its demands. Kon-r's perceptions were colored by the here and now.

"He chose to save both because he could and refused to play my 'game,' holding *me* responsible for their deaths, because I hold the true power of life and death. He chose his own path."

The Warriors were stunned. Who was he to challenge a time-tested, holy tradition? Kon-r considered Cean's reaction to the final test. He had challenged the Angeal's power. What better cause was there than saving the lives of those you loved *and* those who could not protect themselves? So, the problem wasn't the choice he made; the problem was that he refused to play the ancient game. He dared to do something new, to go his own way. He had stood up for what he thought was right and put his life on the line. He had shaken the heavens. In Kon-r's mind, Cean passed the test with flying colors.

A decision was necessary. "Tell me, Warriors of the Hall, past and present, how do you vote? Life or death. Let your blades cast the final vote."

The First studied her long and hard. There was an icy shard of doubt picking at his brain. He couldn't shake the habits of his time, though, so he placed his blade on the table, point menacingly aimed at Mak-Scaire. Each Warrior did the same in rapid order, except one. Kon-r, the last to vote, placed his weapon on the table with the tip facing him, and the pommel facing Cean. That made twelve votes for death and one for life. The Warriors focused on the face of the Angeal.

She was about to render her judgement, to place her own brilliant blade in position, when Kon-r grabbed his weapon and leapt onto the table. He took a position straddling Cean, sword held high, and shouted in defiance, "No! Not this one. Not now. This man was right. We must change, and he is an instrument of change. If you take his life, you'll have to take mine first. I will save him, if I can." He hoped the Angeal understood. The other Warriors tensed, waiting for the Cath Angeal's orders to attack. What else could she say?

The Angeal was considering the same question. Kon-r was not a flighty individual. Kon-r's statement was like waving a red flag in front of the others, but it was a warning aimed at her, too. The island nation would be a memory within months. What would Cean do? Where would he go, if anywhere? She knew that Kon-r's end was near. He had seen it too, although the details were obscured.

If the Warrior tradition was to continue, it would have to be with Cean, and not on this island. The fisherman's son would have to grow up fast, take what he could from the past, and struggle into an uncertain future. The Dark would be planning and acting, too, both here and abroad. One side never existed long without the other. The

Cath Angeal was staggeringly powerful as universal beings go, but she wasn't omniscient; she wasn't all-powerful. She couldn't control the men that create the future, nor could she control the ramifications of their actions. She had lost battles before; she had lost entire planetary systems to the Darkness—millions of people cut off from the Light, never to be heard from again. But she had never been rebuffed by an individual, as she had been by Cean.

"Why can't we try to save them all?" asked Cean. Honestly, she couldn't answer. Why did some die while others lived? She could see, after having spent centuries with these people of flesh and blood, that the answer might not be the food and drink humanity needed. The answer was faith, faith in the Power of Light, faith in the idea that all was as it should be. She could accept that. It was her nature. But humans were wild cards.

She pointed at Kon-r. "You have linked yourself to this boy, for better or worse. Are you ready to suffer the consequences of your choice?" Kon-r shifted his weight and weapon, anticipating the worst. Yet he smiled, and her heart broke again.

"Yes, Angeal; I am ready." He bowed to each Warrior, a sign of respect and friendship. Before he could act, she pointed at Cean, who floated higher over the table, out of Kon-r's reach and out of harm's way.

She cried in a voice that shook the Hall, a voice that echoed through the Ban Castlean. "Behold! A Knight of the Light, Warrior of the future, Protector of Right, and he who has become the hope of this world. I rename thee Dochas: the hope of our cause." A brilliant flash of blue fire filled the hall, and a new Warrior found himself standing at the Table of Law, covered in a full suit of gleaming white armor, a flaming, silver sword in his right hand, a tall banner-spear in his left, and a large circular shield strapped to his back. His wounds vanished, and Cean Mak-Scaire stood tall and straight, his eyes smoldering with power and determination. The banner he held depicted a white tree crowned with seven silver stars. The banner glowed with a vitality of its own. The blazing stars lit the hall as the Warriors looked on in wonder and took strength from that light. The tree and stars had never been seen in that world, but they had a long, glorious history, filled with heartbreak and joy. The Cath Angeal shed tears of happiness, remembering those who fought under this banner. Hope would light the way.

chapter 20:

COMMAND

Torven Lok had a full cargo of food from the Inland Sea, and he had to find a port and a buyer. Before he could do that, he had to determine which port would give him the best chance to get in and out with his money, his ship, and the lives of his crew. He stood in his cabin as the *Ban Colm* sailed west by southwest after passing the Pillars of Heaven, the western gateway to the Inland Sea. The *Ban Colm* had been lucky on this trip, sailing through the strait without wind or water concerns, without pirate attack.

Lok's cabin was solid, simple, and comfortable. A tall man, Lok could stand up straight in the small space. The back wall of his room, set over the keel, looked out onto the ocean, a series of windows allowing sunlight and air into his quarters. Above his head was a large skylight made of a huge piece of quartz crystal the crew had found on one of the eastern islands of the South Sea. Tor loved his crystal innovation and had rewarded the carpenter and blacksmith for their brilliant work in shaping and placing the crystal.

The rest of the cabin was crafted of exotic hardwoods from every corner of the known world. He understood the pride of the solid craftsman who turned his work into artistry, utilitarian beauty. He felt the same pleasure driving the *Ban Colm* through rough seas and high winds, reveling in his ship and his ability to drive her. Tor gazed over the ocean trail left by the *Ban Colm*, a watery comet's tail. It was all one, really. The carpenter, blacksmith, and ship's captain testing themselves against the demands of their crafts, striving to be the best, to express themselves through their work. Their efforts said, *See what I have made; see what I can do. This is who I am, and I am unique.*

He smiled. Not often did his mind work in this manner. The sea and his crew demanded constant attention. Philosophizing, as any good Gardei would tell you, will get you killed. *I must be getting old.* Sometimes, on a lonely, quiet night watch, when he walked the deck, listening to the sea and wind in the rigging, Tor would reflect on his life, the choices he had made, the costs of those decisions. He would wonder what a family might have been like, where he would meet his end. But those thoughts were allowed under the stars, walking and thinking alone. He needed a friendly port of call, where he would find a haven for his crew. He needed a plan; his people expected one. He would not fail them.

Tor had to find a way to get paid. Without money, he couldn't provision and re-arm his ship, and if he couldn't do that, escape would be impossible. He pulled out a well-used map of Athlan and the four outer islands. He was sailing southwest by south, meaning he would approach Athlan from its northeastern corner, and the outer island of Nord-at-Ost. As soon as the watchkeepers of the tower on the island spied his ship, they would flash signals to the mainland less than three sea miles away. There were two major ports on the sheltered eastern cost of Athlan: Krastene toward the north, and Cala toward the south. Each port was sheltered from the westerly winds. Both could handle his ship and its cargo, but both might prove dangerous to anyone carrying food, given the state of the island and the people on it. The other danger was to the ship itself. Who wouldn't want his ship? Who didn't want to flee doomed Athlan? What if he and his people were overwhelmed by thousands of panicked citizens desperate to escape?

He needed information. Tor decided to pick a small crew and land them somewhere to get the lay of the land. Would it be Krastene or Cala? No difference in harbor, really, but who did he know? Who would give him the information he needed to pull this off? He had friends in all of the Athlan ports, but would they still be there? Could he really trust them in life-and-death circumstances? Krastene was the better port facility, but Cala had a better reputation with traders. Military supplies? That was anyone's guess. Rumor was only Gardei armories contained what he needed; all other weapons caches had been plundered by roving bands or marauders. He'd have to see for himself.

And where was the Marfach Gardei? What was Kon-r doing to hold things together? Tor walked around the table and stood before the rear windows. He watched the water carving made by the keel collapse on itself and dissolve into sparkling diamond droplets. Kon-r, last Warrior of Athlan—would he ever see him again? *Probably not*, he thought. *Our paths separated years ago*. He couldn't imagine the load on his friend's shoulders now. How would he wield the Gardei, and against whom would he fight? How would he keep order? Whatever happened, Kon-r wouldn't abandon the people of Athlan, nor would he walk away from the Gardei; he couldn't. Of all the men he had fought with, lived with, laughed and cried with, Kon-r Sighur was the only man Torven Lok recognized as his superior. He knew in his heart he would rather die fighting next to Kon-r than anyone else, present crew included. Tor felt an overwhelming sadness.

He had once heard that after a certain age, one stopped thinking about new challenges and started to concentrate on doing the things he forgot to do or should have done. He felt like that now. He felt a hole in his life, a nagging emptiness, a terrible anxiety that screamed to him and scratched across the softness of his soul. *You left him and ran out on your brothers.* He thought it was the right thing to do at the time, but at the possible end of all things Athlan, his self-doubt came crashing down on his weakened psyche. Had all of this—his ship, his life—been a simple attempt to run away from his responsibilities?

Kon-r had absolved him from his Gardei oath: "Those who can serve, must serve." But had Tor forgiven himself? *I would like one more fight next to him, shields locked together, muscles straining against the common enemy. Love, hate, fear, anger—all emotions compressed, directed with awesome power down the shaft of my spear.* He wanted to listen to the roar of battle, the roar of life and death, and then experience victory and overwhelming relief when it was over, the enemy broken and dead at their feet. Standing once more—alive, young, and laughing. *One more time would be very good,* he thought.

He listened to the sea slapping against the white hull. He heard gulls cry overhead, a forlorn sound, and he realized he was becoming an old fool. His skittering mind got back to the problem: they would sail within rowing distance of Cala in two nights' time. Avoiding harbor patrols, he would go ashore with Rok Tan and the gig's crew during the late watch. Tor would try to contact Vespex Kee, a wounded Marine Gardei Quartermaster, retired from the service, who was now a minor trader in naval supplies, but, more importantly, a major trader in information. Was Vespex alive? Who knew? He kept an office and warehouse two blocks up Dragon Street, just above the major wharf, and a home in a rise overlooking the harbor. If anyone really knew what was going on, it would be Vespex.

As a sergeant in the Marine Gardei, he had had the reputation as the man to see if one wanted anything out of the ordinary. Vespex's saving grace was that he was hell on wheels in a fight. Short and squat, but enormously muscled, he could not be moved once he took his place in the line of battle. With a low center of gravity and tremendous strength and quickness, hidden behind a Gardei shield and armed with either spear or sword, he was a frightening opponent. He was still a formidable killer, even without his left hand. In the end, the deterrent of violence had kept him alive and relatively well. Hopefully, luck and his nasty reputation would continue to protect him.

Seoult and KT would command the ship while he was gone. They would sail east over the horizon and come back on the late tide of the second night, flying three lanterns from the main mast, one white and two red. Tor would guide the crew back to the ship. He would instruct Seoult to return the following night if they didn't arrive on time. If, after the third night, Tor and crew were still nowhere to be found, KT and Seoult must assume he and Rok Tan were dead. Under no circumstances was the *Ban Colm* to be put in danger. It was to be sailed around Athlan, and KT was to try to reach Kon-r Sighur and offer their services to the Marfach Gardei.

Tor felt sure Kon-r would treat her right. If not, their fate was their own, and KT would be captain, making the final decisions. Tor shuffled through his charts and selected a half dozen that he would review with KT and Seoult. They would decide on a destination for the *Ban Colm* and its people if an alliance with Kon-r was not possible.

CHAPTER 21:

MONSTERS

Celine closed her mind to the chaos she had created. While the women in the glade vented their anguish and frustration, she retreated under a large pine with her back against the rough bark and reviewed what had been happening to her since she had taken her husband's life. Her first vision of evil had shaken her to her core. Initially, the intruder had grabbed control of her mind, threatening her sanity. But she had regained control. In fact, she had thrown the dark power out of her mind altogether. She escaped with her children and then left them with her sister, Alesia. She had listened and taken her kids, but Alesia had believed her sister had gone crazy. Killing her husband and abandoning her children? What mother did that? Celine left them all and moved inland, spreading the word that the Sisters had to meet at the old *oake* glade near the bend of the Shining River, just above small village of Botley. But she moved as if in a deep, black fog. She had left her boys and girls behind. She felt quite certain that she would never see them again—never hug them, never listen to them laugh, never tuck them in at night, nor watch them grow. She hurt so much. What compulsion made her destroy her life and theirs?

Walking along, she would find herself in tears, not knowing how long she cried, unaware of where she had walked. How would they remember her—the woman who'd abandoned them? Her heart broke over and over, the pieces getting smaller and smaller. She knew there would always be a hole in her soul—an emptiness that would eventually engulf her into oblivion. She had left so fast—a final hug and meaningless words. "You'll be alright. Mama will be right back for you. Do what Alesia tells you." And she was gone.

There was a power directing her; she had no will of her own. Celine was dead to the world. Her children, her life, herself—left behind. Yet she struggled on, trying to find meaning, trying to figure out what had changed her fundamental humanity. That she now had a purpose, one she did not comprehend, was clear. But whose purpose, and why was she chosen to fulfill it?

When the sun soared in the sky, she would sit down in an open, isolated spot and try to exercise her mind. At first, she didn't know what she expected. How could she get to that place again, where she could see the other being? She wondered whether she could do "other things" with what she called her "power." Little by little, she learned her abilities, some quite accidentally. In Jarsberg, a small farming community, she walked through the village green in her usual dark daze, lost in thought, her life in turmoil. Looking up in the middle of the town square, she realized that today was market day. Market day was a day of fun in the small villages of Athlan. People met to talk about their neighbors, the weather, their farms, and whatever else crossed their minds came up. The young ran between stalls, laughing and screaming for sweets, while livestock made lowing noises behind butcher tents. Chickens ran between the feet of villagers and children as dogs chased them. Even though Athlan was crumbling, market day remained important to powerless people.

Celine tried to take everything in, and as she did, she saw a large, rough-looking man steal an apple from an old woman's cart. He began to walk away, whistling a merry tune. Celine became angry; in fact, her state of mind changed from slightly dazed traveler to incensed woman. The thief stood for every man, including her dead husband, who brazenly ignored the basic rules of good conduct—the heart of the Sisters' values. Her world turned red. She clenched her hands and jaws and silently screamed, *Stop, thief!* The rogue—a large, well-built man—immediately froze mid-stride, lost his balance, and fell. He couldn't even get his arms and hands in front of his body to break his fall. His face simply buried itself into the dusty earth. His nose cracked, and blood flowed heavily into the dirt and into his open mouth. He gagged.

Celine gasped, not sure if she had caused his collapse. She waited for him to get up. It didn't happen right away. Slowly, he pushed himself from the dusty ground, spit blood and dust from his mouth, brushed off his clothes, looked around furtively, and began to walk away, faster than before. His head swiveled in all directions as he fled. She waited, watched him go, calmed herself, and silently said again, relatively calmly, *Stop, thief!* Her anger had been diminished by her shock. Nothing happened; he continued on his way, weaving through the carts and tents, no doubt looking for something else to steal. She followed, closed the gap between them, and with him in her direct line of sight, thought again, *Stop, thief!* The man, leaning over a smoking brazier covered with pork ribs, lost control of his limbs and collapsed on top of it. Food flew everywhere, and hot coals landed on the ground and on his back. Smoke and sparks flew up as if they were an offering to the heavens. The thief, unable to move or make a sound, lay mute on the ground as coals burned through his greasy tunic. Just as his hair began to smolder, people arrived with buckets of water and put out all the small fires that were burning around, under, and on him. Smoke rose from his clothing. People helped him to his feet, not knowing something extraordinary had just happened.

He studied the crowd with wide, panicked eyes. He was confused, angry, and embarrassed. People were laughing as they retold the story of the big, clumsy lout who fell into the charcoal brazier and began to cook along with the pig. A large, athletic man, he knew something was wrong. Something had been done to him, and he searched the crowd for the culprit. His eyes met hers. She was standing by a flower vendor's cart. He recognized her from earlier that day, when he took the apple. She was still behind him. His eyes narrowed, and he weaved between the carts and tents; she couldn't see him. Celine knew she was in trouble. He could come from anywhere, and even if she called for help, he would still be on her before help arrived. She saw him getting closer, beside the large vegetable tent. She recognized her husband's mad eyes in the thief's face. She tried not to panic. Breathing deep, eyes locked on his, she waited until he approached. She thought one word, *Stop*. He stopped cold. His face twisted as he desperately tried to move. She could see the anguish in his face, a wild animal caught and powerless. She thought, *Sit*. He sat. Tears rolled down his face. As if to a dog, condescendingly she said, *Stay*. And he stayed, hate visible in his eyes, his body no longer his own. Celine stared for a moment, shocked again by what she had done. She had controlled a human being as if he was a mindless thrall. Not only that, she had enjoyed humiliating him. She turned on her heels and walked away from him and Jarsberg, not sure who was more evil, the thief who stole the apple or the thief who stole a man's body and mind.

She tried to stay off the main roads but couldn't express why. She didn't know where she was going. She knew she was in danger. She worried about her anger. It came on so fast and was all-consuming. The word *passion* came to mind, as she reviewed how she felt when she first controlled the thief. Celine realized she felt both good and bad when she exerted her power. She felt that her actions were right and wrong at the same time. She experimented with her ability as she walked. She tried to make small objects, like stones or twigs, move from her path. That didn't work. Then she tried to communicate with cows in a field: no success. Birds, a smaller target, ignored her mental commands. She came to a stream, little more than ankle deep, as it cut through pastureland, and the water ran cold over her feet. As a lark, she tried to bend the water around her feet. She failed. Then she concentrated on a curved, imaginary brick wall protecting her legs from the flowing water. The water began to flow around the mental wall, and the stream bed became rocky and dry under her feet. She caught her breath and furtively looked around to see if anyone had witnessed her trick. No one had. She released the image of the wall. The stream immediately resumed its course over her feet and around her ankles. Celine didn't know whether to laugh or cry. What was happening to her? She gathered her wet tunic and climbed up onto the bank, sat down on the grass, spread her shift out in the sun, and considered what she had learned over the last few days.

She could control the mind, and therefore the actions, of a man, but only up to a certain distance. She couldn't move objects with her mind, but she could deflect things away from her body, as the stream had proven. Still, these talents were secondary to what she felt was her real power: the ability to see things or people—or at least one very evil person. And did she really have that power? Or had it happened once, and that was that? Celine closed her eyes, listening to the water and feeling the sun. Her mind roamed unfettered, seeking nothing. She began to see random scenes, strange visions—some clear, some cloudy, none of which she could interpret. Bands of people moving across Athlan, wind ships sailing from what she felt was a faraway country, a boy and girl holding hands in a strange land, faceless men standing back to back, weapons in their hands. She felt happy and sad as the images passed. Maybe later, when she had time to think about things, her visions would clarify.

She had travelled out of herself again; she had seen things, although she didn't know what they meant. She had not seen what she had begun to call the Evil One. He remained elusive, and that didn't bother her. Celine opened her eyes and there, directly across the small brook, was a tall man dressed in black, a carved staff pointed at her. Behind him were hundreds of men and boys, all armed with an odd collection of weapons adapted farm tools, staring at her as if she was their next meal. Celine could feel the tension in the air. Physically, she could feel him across the water. His staff seemed to radiate a band of power that connected them somehow. She didn't move.

Seconds stretched into minutes and imagined hours before his thoughts crashed into her mind. *He has been searching for you....Celine, yes, Celine. You have hidden well, woman, but now I have found you, and through me, he knows you.* She could barely breathe. He had violated her just as she had violated the thief, as the Evil One had violated her earlier. The man in black tilted his head, as if receiving a message or listening to something. His eyes refocused on her. *You will come with me*. A large group of men began to cross the stream, and Celine felt a tremendous pressure clamping her skull like a vice. She screamed. She couldn't think. The ragged men were in the water, moving as one. Her assailant stood rooted to the far bank. He smiled; evil radiated from his body, a red nimbus surrounding him, making his form waver as she fought to regain control. She concentrated, gritting her teeth, her body tense, each muscle straining to break free from the pain and compulsion. Beads of sweat and blood broke out on her forehead. Slowly, oh so slowly, she raised her right hand, wanting to repulse the evil, to stop the pressure. As she moved her arm and clenched her hand, blood welled up from the cuts her nails made in her palms and the red color around her opponent began to fade. She was gaining control, she could feel it, and the men in the stream slowed their crossing. Her determination grew. She seemed to take power from the earth, drawing it from the green grass through her body into her seething mind; she directed the force toward her enemy.

Celine couldn't believe how calm she was. She watched him and the men in the stream. She had no intention of going with them, no intention of letting them touch her. Her anger built up, her vision sharpened, time slowed. She raised her hand, palm outward, and the men in the water fell into the stream, unable to right themselves. They began to drown in gently flowing, shallow water. She looked into the eyes of Devilman. *Yes, you are Devilman,* she said to him. *Your time has come to an end. Tell your master, if you can.* Speaking these words, Celine closed her open palm into a tight fist and thrust it out at Devilman, as if she were trying to punch him. An invisible, compact block of power shot across the water. Devilman's head snapped back, her power pounding him between the eyes. Devilman flew back through the air and fell senseless to the ground, his once red, burning eyes wide open and milky white. He did not breathe. The remaining men and boys, seeing their leader powerless, dropped their weapons, broke, and ran. Celine stretched her mind toward the prone Devilman, searching for signs of life. There were none. She eased herself off the ground. The shallow rill washed over and around fifteen bodies, fifteen men who had been controlled by Devilman, fifteen normal people forced to do evil's bidding against their own will: all dead because of her. A languid hand flowed with the light current. Loose clothing billowed in clear water. Long hair, human seaweed, reached for her. Relaxed, the bodies seemed to be sleeping. She couldn't look any longer. She shivered and quickly marched away from this place of death.

Again, she asked herself, *Who is the monster here?* Twice she had used her power of control, and twice she had enjoyed it. This time she had killed. She was no longer Celine. That woman was long gone. She thought of herself as Sister Celine, and she had a job to do, but she didn't know why, and she was afraid to consider what her end would be. She felt like crying but couldn't. In the warm sunlight, she walked away cold as marble.

chapter 22:

Reborn Green

Celine wandered through neglected fields and over roads congested with other wanderers. She was unaware of her direction, yet always moving. To say that she was in shock after killing more than fifteen people would not be quite accurate. She was, more than anything, shut down to almost everything around her. She ate very little and drank only when she found herself near running water. Her clothes were covered in dust, stained by the grass she slept on and the mud she walked through. Her long hair was tangled and dirty.

She was trying to see her new self, and she couldn't get a clear picture. Her "self" was shattered beyond repair, and it was as if a thousand disjointed parts of "her" moved loosely, aimlessly through the day. Light, wind, and heat passed through her inconsequential self, meeting no resistance. Celine couldn't understand why she just didn't blow away. That would be an easy end to the nightmare of her life.

Dragging her feet listlessly through the dry dust of a country farm road, she looked left and saw a perfectly plowed farmer's field. Row after perfect row stretched toward a low ridge of hills to the west. The sky was a wonderful blue canopy above a fertile brown field with perfect furrows that would never be planted or harvested. In the center of the field was one tall green tree filled with birds and song. The tree connected the land and sky. Celine was drawn to the tree. She left the road, walking across the field. She had to get to it. As she approached, she saw a small sunken area of earth filled with lush grass, yellow and blue wildflowers, and low bushes covered with red berries. In the center of the dale, there was a crystal-clear pool. The entire area was invisible from the road. As she walked toward the pool, she seemed to disappear into the inviting earth.

She felt like she stood at the center of the earth, as if she had come home, as if she could stay there the rest of her life. Standing on the edge of the clear water, she removed her clothes and let them fall around her feet. Naked, she entered the fresh water and submerged. It was surprisingly deep, and her worries, guilt, and all of her pain washed away. She remained under water as long as she could. Her eyes were wide open; she was in a world of shadows and saw leaves shimmer above the water. Celine watched her past fade into meaningless memories. Her limbs floated, weightless. Her hair billowed around her head, reaching for the sky. Peace. Celine needed air but didn't want to move, didn't want to bear the weight of her life. Deliberately, she pushed the air out of her lungs and breathed in cold water. This would be it, she thought; this would be a fine ending.

She waited, her feet firmly resting on smooth stones that lined the bottom of the pool. Nothing changed, other than the fact that she was no longer breathing, and that meant that everything had changed. She panicked. She screamed, trying to release her soul. Not dying was worse than dying, which is what she had hoped for. Deep laughter filled her mind. Celine whipped her head around, twisting her hair around her head. She couldn't see anyone, yet the laughter continued, low and deep, and power rumbled in her chest and head. *I didn't bring you this far to watch you die, young mother.* Hearing the voice, Celine stood helpless, waiting. *Come out of the water, Celine, we have things to discuss.*

She swam to the surface and climbed onto the grassy bank. Celine turned toward the voice, a real voice, and saw, or thought she saw, a large woman sitting on the other side of the pool. The woman's image was unstable. She shimmered as if she was looking through a curtain of heat. Celine sat, rigid, cross-legged, naked, dripping, and bewildered. She tried to see the woman more clearly but could not. Instead, she saw a shifting reality that resembled many women of all shapes and sizes. Celine could feel her power. She could feel it in her bones, and she knew she sat there, lungs full of water, not breathing yet still alive, because of that presence.

Relax, Celine. You are safe now. The first part of your journey is over. Before we discuss the things to come, you will be transformed. Celine tried to move, she tried to scream, terrified.

Transformed? Transformed into what? Celine knew that her old "self" was long gone. But to be changed against one's will? *No.* She could not accept that. She would not accept that. *I must fight!* She tried to focus her mind on the power across from her. Maybe she could control her mind, if only she could....

No, child. The powers you have discovered are my gift to you. They are but thin imitations of myself. You have no power, unless I give it to you. She surrendered and prepared for whatever was to come. She had already thrown one life away, of what import was another? *Come, come, it's not that bad, Celine. I understand. You are confused. Your children, they are gone. Your life, it is gone. You sit there as dead as you are alive.*

Your bodily functions, for the most part, have stopped. Your mind is still alive, but movement is impossible. Her voice was hypnotic: low and slow and immensely powerful. The voice rumbled across the pond and seemed to enter Celine from the ground. She could feel it move steadily through her body. She didn't try to move. She didn't want to. She had no desire to do or think anything.

Passively, calmly, she watched the woman spread her arms wide, and Celine thought her arms enclosed the entire dale, but that could not be. She began to feel pressure on her skin, as if the slight power of sunlight was gently caressing her. She was not uncomfortable. She also thought she saw the flowers and bushes nearby growing, extending their branches and stems toward her. She thought she saw the great tree's roots burrow under the surface of the earth toward her. The pool seemed to expand until her feet were covered with water.

Do not be alarmed, Celine. I have chosen you. What happens next is for the best. Celine's sense of well-being deepened as the words resonated within her. Slowly, so as not to alarm her, Celine's body began to bleed. Red trickled from all openings, all pores. Blood gathered into rivulets and ran off her body, creating a red cloud in the pool. She watched her own passing in contented silence. Her only thought was how beautiful the red strands looked against her white skin, amidst the yellow and blue flowers, against the bright green grass. Although calm, she felt the deep sadness of those who have lost something precious, knowing that they would never get it back, knowing they would never be the same. An invisible hand pushed her forward from the waist, and the water in her lungs erupted from her mouth, returning to the now red pool. Hands gently lowered her onto her back. She was an empty husk of a woman: no breath, no desires, no thoughts, and no real life. Her eyes stared into the mottled green leaves of the great tree, and beyond, she saw small scraps of the endless blue sky. Subtle warmth began to invade her body as the roots of the great tree wrapped her in a strong cocoon. The plants in the dale, including the lush green grass, began to cover the cocoon until all that was visible was a grassy knoll. Celine had been swallowed by the earth. The great tree seemed to slide into the dale, lowering its branches. Even the mound disappeared. Celine was no more.

In the tomb, however, the body of the woman once known as Celine was regenerating. Moisture from the earth saturated her pores. Something akin to human blood, called earth's blood in long lost stories, began to flow into her veins. She burned inside. Her mind became a whirling cloud of bright lights. She could breathe, and her organs worked, but nothing was the same. She felt as if she was part of the earth, part of the great tree. Strength flowed through her toughened form. She could sense the bedrock far below and feel the wind blowing above ground. The sun's warmth penetrated her earthen grave, and she knew exactly where the bright ball sat in the sky. She could feel the cool water in the pool, and she knew she could draw that life-giving fluid directly into her body. Life force hummed all around her, and she felt in tune with her surroundings. *What? Nature?*

She knew she was home. She was safe. She was where she was supposed to be, and she could not separate herself from the dirt and plant life that surrounded her. There was no distinction. She *was* the earth. It was this thought that opened the floodgates of her mind. She could feel the woman across the pool. She could feel her breathing, her heartbeat. She understood that she was the earth, she was that woman. *Yes, little one. You are no longer alone. We are one. Arise and learn what you have become.*

Tree roots receded into the earth. Plants resumed their original positions. Effortlessly, Celine sat up and looked across the pond, strength flowing through her limbs. She knew audible speech was no longer necessary. She could communicate mentally. *With everyone?*

No, sister, not with anyone. You can talk to me and the others you will recruit, but your ability to do this will be limited by their receptiveness, by how attuned they are with the earth. Most people will not hear you. The few who have a true love of the earth will.

Celine considered the word "recruit." What did that mean? But there were so many other questions in her head that she put that one aside and asked the three questions that burned her mind. *Who or what are you, what have you done to me, and why me?*

I'll answer the third first, Celine. I became aware of you when you killed your husband. You killed him because he had to be killed. The act of murder shocked you deeply, but you did what you had to. I felt your resolve and your pain. I picked you because I have decided that I can no longer remain aloof from the affairs of humans. I need a method for intervening when I see the need. I can do many, many things, but I cannot decide on the affairs of humans. I have lived with that limitation since the beginning of time. To influence humanity, I first had to find a human of great resolve who was capable of murder, if necessary. I had to find a person whose aggression was of a defensive nature, geared to protect instead of destroy. You, who had just killed her husband, are one of the few who encompasses both ends of the spectrum: you nurture life as a Sister, and you can destroy life. You are life and death, as am I. Celine, in you, I have created a staff of power that from this day forward will, I hope, play a very significant role in the salvation of our planet.

Celine didn't hold back. *You stole my children from me. You destroyed my life. And now you want me to, what, thank you? Other than the obvious power you have, what gives you the right to take my life and make me into some kind of tool to suit your purpose?* Even as she thought the words, she could feel her connection to the earth. She could feel the new strength in her body and mind. Her veins throbbed with the power of life, and she felt indestructible. She was torn between tears of rage for her lost past and waves of delight as the incredible power of life coursed through her veins.

She wondered if she was human anymore. *Yes and no,* answered the being across the small water. *Yes, you are human becuase you could, if you chose and I allowed it, still breed with a human male. The offspring would be less than human and more. You are not human in the physical change I have put you through. You are more in tune with the earth and all that is natural than any human could be. You will be the stuff of legend on my earth.*

Celine considered the new information. Sitting in the grotto, she was amazed by the abundance of life in this small space. She was surrounded by joy. *Who are you?* thought Celine

My name is Gaiea, for what that is worth, and you won't believe who or what I am.

Chapter 23:

GAME OF STONES

Celine thought, *What do you mean?*

What I mean, daughter, is that there are many powers in the universe, and no one knows how they came to be or how they fit together, or where we will end. Each of us, however, has enormous abilities within our own realm. For all intents and purposes, humans look upon us as gods.

Celine didn't know what to ask first. Her mind was a jumble, but she felt as if she, too, had become a plant, no more than another plant in the glade, perfect and at ease. She asked, *Again, who are you and what have you done to me?*

Gaiea replied, *I will tell you. Please pay attention, for I will not repeat myself. The universe is larger and older than you can comprehend. If I say something happened ten years ago, you can comprehend that. If*

I say it happened one hundred years ago, you still understand. If I say something occurred ten thousand years ago, you understand the concept, but the actual time frame means little. If I say I became a sentient power five billion years ago, what does that mean to you? It is a meaningless number to you, but for me, it is nothing more than my life. When this world was formed, I was here. The world is me, and I am the world. We are separate, yet we are one. The world, in short, is mine. I am the sea. I am the mountains, the air, and the fire at the center of all things. And yet, I exist also as an entity apart from the physical earth. And there are many like me throughout the universe, beings inseparable from planets and stars. We are neither male nor female. We are powers unto ourselves and answer to no force within this universe. We do not travel across the stars; we are the stars and have no need to wander. I have nurtured my earth for billions of years and have created and destroyed things beyond your imagination.

Are you a god? she asked.

Gaiea chuckled, and Celine's body vibrated. *Am I a god? Well, that depends on how you define god. On earth, I have unlimited power in all things except two—time and humanity. I cannot alter time, and I did not create humanity, nor can I eradicate them from my planet. Further, I cannot bend them to my will. In fact, I have tried both, and some force un-*

known to me nullifies my power. They are different in some way. I saw the possibility of their arrival as I watched various forms of life develop over the millennia. In every case, except one, humanity did not evolve. Other forms of life approximating humanity did. In fact, many intelligent life forms have raised themselves to the top of the food chain and considered the planet theirs, but in time they have always fallen back into the earth and been forgotten. But they grew as part of the earth, as a direct result of the natural growth of things and contained no parts that were not of this earth and, therefore, of me. I did not interfere in their development; I didn't tinker with their parts. They evolved as they would, and I watched the beauty of the process. I was content with the outcomes, whatever they were, because they were perfect in their simplicity and natural design.

To Celine, it seemed that Gaiea sat for a moment in thought, and all life in the dale waited, breathless, for her to continue. *Well,* she began, *the process repeated itself more times than I can tell you. Some forms of life recreated themselves on a regular basis because theirs was a superior design, and I always waited for them to achieve a breakthrough that would allow them to advance to the next stage in their growth, whatever that may have been, but it never happened.*

Celine was enthralled by her narrative; she sat still as stone and images flooded her mind. She began to see the creatures that the Being saw in her own mind. *Giant beings with active brains and great determination could not get beyond tribal wars and, eventually, wiped themselves out. Water creatures who could think and build lived deep in the seas and created a world without air, and they ruled the seas in strength and joy, but they, too, were destroyed by a new breed of predator that hunted in packs and were large and powerful. Quick, furtive creatures running on all fours learned to predict the movements of the stars, but couldn't learn to protect their families from even more clever predators that had brains the size of walnuts, but learned how to spread a disease the superior race had no defense against. Mathematical and martial civilizations came and went, always with some basic flaw that kept them chained to a disastrous future. I have seen cities built and witnessed battles of such beauty and depravity that you could not fathom them, even though you have lived your life here on this glorious piece of rock.* And Celine did see them, and she felt their joy and the sadness of their passing. She felt their hope and their despair. She saw beauty and life and wept before its destruction. *I have been feared by millions, worshipped, and given sacrifices, although I've never shown myself, nor have I asked for adulation. I need it not, yet they need to give it.*

She continued. *But something happened to a fairly standard design that had repeated itself many times in many places. Tree climbers who also walked the savannahs looking for food developed as family groups. Societies came together. Farming was born when larger groups could no longer live on game from local areas—all standard. But this race developed a strong self-awareness. They separated themselves from other animals and saw themselves as the masters of the land. They began to focus on daily needs and their physical and spiritual futures. These "people," as they called themselves, began to worship gods, gods who lived beyond this earth, in the ether. They developed the concepts they still call "good" and "evil."*

Gaiea was still. Celine sat in stunned silence. Life stretched back billions of years, lives just like hers. Beings who resembled fish and lizards and furred creatures in trees: all just like her, with families, fear, and joy, with pain and anxiety for their children and loved ones. She had seen terrible cataclysms—floods that destroyed air-breathing life, volcanoes that blotted out the sun, wiping the planet clean; earthquakes that swallowed entire continents and folded them neatly beneath the ocean floor. Celine knew that Gaiea was responsible for all of it in some way, whether she actively caused everything to happen or simply let it go, knowing nature would follow its course.

Yes, little one. I could have changed things. I haven't because there is no need. Whatever happens is supposed to happen. If temperatures were

to drop severely tomorrow and ice covered everything to the north of us,
millions would die. But what of that? They will return over time, or not.
Other beings will take their place, eventually, and I will be just as content
because the natural process continues.

Celine considered her words. *Is Athlan doomed to destruction?*

Yes, it is.

Celine sobbed. *Would you not even try to save innocent people?*

The other voice boomed in Celine's mind. *Especially not to save*
people, and none of them are innocent.

Celine heard something new in the Earth Being's voice. There
was passion, an intensity that made Celine shiver. *What do you have*
against the people of Athlan?

Child, have you not heard anything? Have you not understood what
I have told you? My province is the entire earth, Celine. There are millions
and millions of "people" on the face of my planet, yet I DID NOT PUT
THEM HERE. THEY ARE NOT PART OF ME AND SHOULD
NOT EXIST.

If not you, who put them here? Celine noticed it had become dark.
Time no longer seems to matter.

But Gaiea disagreed. *Time does matter, Celine, because it is not of my making. Who or what compels all beings to march to time's beat? Why? Tell me, child.*

The implication is that something controls time and in so doing, exerts control over you and everyone and everything on earth.

Exactly: who or what controls time? And it isn't just control of earth, Celine; it is control of the universe. What could control the entire universe, using time as the tool? People represent a mystery that is the other side of the coin of time. People are different. They are of this world, and they are not.

How do you know, Mother?

When a tree dies in the forest, it comes back to me—all of it. There is nothing missing. It is me returning to myself—what has left returns. But when people die and are returned to the earth, or they are burnt and their ashes are scattered, something is missing. I can sense it, although I cannot tell you what it is. But there is a void, a hollow spot, and every person who is put into the ground or sea or air has this hollow spot, and I do not know what once filled it. I do know that what is missing was never me.

Celine felt very small. She caught a glimpse of an immense universe and understood that vast powers were at work, powers that neither she, nor even Mother, fully understood. *What does it all mean, Mother?*

Child, open your mind to me. We need to leave this place. Celine calmed her whirling brain and felt a presence grab her consciousness. She found herself standing in the sun atop Creogh Radahar, with Earth Mother next to her. There were the meeting table and chairs of the Four, empty. They walked to the edge of the platform and looked out over the smoking plain of Athlan. Celine saw things differently. Her vision was augmented by a sense of right and wrong, as she knew those terms in her past life. She could see the fires and rents in the earth; she could also see groups of people far below. Many groups moved randomly, as if lost, and indeed, they were. But there were other groups that seemed to move with a purpose, and, as she observed the island, she found many groups moving toward Creogh Radahar from all directions. Almost all felt "bad" to her. She sensed the red of desperation and anger in these cadres. There was one small group, however, coming up from the coast in the far southeastern part of the island, and this group felt different. Celine sensed desperation but determination, and cool dark green settled over her as she perceived the sensation of "good."

What am I seeing, Mother? Gaiea stood still on the mountain top. Her eyes were closed, but she saw farther and deeper than Celine. She saw the workings of the inner earth and knew to the second how long this mountaintop had left on earth. She saw the tribes of the earth seething like malignant growths on every land mass. She saw ships on her sea sailing toward Athlan and wondered why humans would sail toward their own destruction.

Celine, I have told you that there are powers other than me, powers that roam the universe?

Yes.

And I have told you about the human concepts of good and evil?

Yes, Mother, you have.

Many of the powers that roam the heavens consider themselves to be good or evil. The beings are implacably opposed to one another. They have fought across time and space since the beginning. Think of that, little one. For ten billion years, these entities have decimated each other, and there is no conclusion in sight. The Great Battle has degenerated into a game of stones; each side tries to control more stones across the gaping void of the universe. These stones are planets, like earth. In order to control the planet, since they cannot control me, they attempt to control the inhabitants of the planet. Here, on earth, the primary inhabitants are human, or people, as we have discussed. The heavenly combatants choose a battleground and begin a campaign to enlist forces that will carry out their will.

Is that what I see out on the plain? Are those the chosen moving to battle?

Yes, child. This is the beginning.

After considering everything she had heard, Celine asked, *Where are the celestial powers? The Travelers? Shouldn't they be here, too?*

Mother smiled. *Yes, Celine, they should be here, and they are. But they cannot take part in this battle, unless they are fighting beings like themselves. On earth, you will see men with special abilities fighting each other while the Travelers fight each other on another plane.*

I still don't understand why this is important to you, Mother. In the end the earth is still yours. Isn't it?

Yes and no. Wherever this battle is fought, after time, the planet takes on the character of the winner. There is nothing I can do to stop the change. If that happens, we become just another stone in the game. Gaiea paused. *We become good or evil and are never free to exert our true nature again. Every planetary power despises the Travelers and their unending battle. They fight, and we pay the price. It is for this reason and this reason alone that you have been created. I will not sit idly waiting for my fate to be determined by others. Like the Travelers, I cannot directly* meddle in these battles. However, like the minions of the Travelers, I have created you as my paladin, and you will recruit women like yourself and remake them in your image, as I have remade you in mine.

chapter 24:

You Shall Kill

Who am I to recruit? Celine was in a particular frame of mind. She no longer considered the situation strange. That she would fight at Mother's direction, or by her side, was an accepted fact. There would be recruits. She simply wanted more information. *Earth Mother, how am I going to battle?* The earth seemed to stand still. Celine felt as if her brain had become part of Mother's. A story unfolded in her head. She saw two lines of men reaching back millions of years. She saw an endless ebb and flow between the men; she saw battles and bloodshed.

Celine couldn't see a clear difference between the warring groups, but she assumed that there was one. Time flashed in her mind: combatants in bright armor slaughtered each other. Entire armies with banners flying murdered and maimed one another. Shadow men struggled quietly in dark places. Faces flashed before her eyes until they blurred.

Yet, in the end, one composite face appeared, and she knew his name: the Warrior. He was young, his expression seemed determined, and he was beautiful.

On the other side, faces rifled past her eyes and a different face emerged. Celine recognized the madness in the eyes, a malevolent lust for destruction: "the Dark" was a phrase that came to mind. *Mother, who are these men?*

Gaiea answered, *We have discussed the Travelers, their battles, and how planets are turned against our will, have we not?*

Yes, Mother.

The men you have seen are the mercenaries of the Travelers. One side represents the "Light," as they call it, the other group fights for the Dark. Can you guess who belongs to what side?

Not difficult, Mother. The young man is the "Light," the other is certainly the "Dark." So, what?

Mother chuckled. *Exactly: so, what? The "so what" is this: others are fighting for control of my planet. And, while we would all do better if the forces of Light prevailed, they may not do so, and even if they did win, I—we—would be less in the end. If they lose, we would eventually be dominated by the Dark. That would not be good either. In fact, it would be much worse. The madness you saw in Dark's eyes would, in the end, be seen in our eyes. In either case, I will not be controlled. Humans, in of all their forms, have been incapable of living together in anything resembling long-term peace. As their civilizations advance, they become more deadly, more dangerous to themselves and my planet. Once they attract the attention of the Travelers, however, their warlike tendencies increase, and they reflect the power and greed of their masters.*

You have asked the right questions, and here are the answers, Celine. You, and those you will select and convert, will have part of my ability to neutralize powers, as I can control my native planet, if I wish. You and your troops will have to decide who you will stand with and who you will resist. As you killed your husband for the benefit of your family, so too shall you battle the powers of those you deem harmful to the earth, and you shall kill, if that action is required to solve the problem. If you must slaughter both sides, do so. In the end, it will be for the best.

Is mine the ultimate power in the coming battle?

No, child. Nothing is certain, and I cannot foretell the future because it, too, is time-driven. I will give you whatever strength I can, but other powers are at play, and you will take your chances in the great battle for earth.

Can I be killed?

No one like you has ever walked the earth. Definitive answers are impossible, but I will not deceive you: I think you can be killed. You will have to fight for our survival, just as they are fighting for theirs. I cannot guarantee your life. I don't know if the power I share will sustain you.

Celine asked, *Will you fight, Mother?*

I will fight in much the same way you will: by trying to resist certain powers. I will try to deny them in ways you cannot comprehend, for mine is the power of the earth, and I create, protect, and endure. Destruction, life and death, are parts of creation, nothing more.

Celine considered Gaiea's words. Stars wheeled in the night sky, and time sped by. Things were so strange, yet curiously normal since her transformation. Waves still crashed against the western shore far below, and the sun would rise in a few hours. She could feel the waves through the bones of the mountain. She could feel the heat of the sun speeding around the curve of the earth.

Alright, then, she murmured. *What do you want me to do?* The Mother considered her words. What should she do? The ancient battle—she always thought she would have more warning, more time to prepare. But faced with the ultimate battle for control of her home, herself, her hopes would be pinned on this fragile tool. What frightened her was that none of her kind had ever stopped the process of conversion, once it started. Using this woman was a unique strategy, never before tried on any planet by Caretakers, which is what beings like her called themselves. The reason was simple: no Caretaker wanted to give up control of their planet. No Caretaker believed anyone or anything could do a better job of protecting what was theirs. It was called pride. A human concept, but pride, arrogance, greed—were not these also the values of the major powers in the universe? Was she any different than they? In some ways, no, but in an essential way, yes. She did not care to dominate other planets. She was content with her own domain. Was it all a matter of degree?

Mother extended her senses into the earth and drew strength from her planet. She sighed. She could lose this orb. She could become a tool of the Travelers. She would be nothing but an old, defeated power, soon to be dominated and forgotten. No! She would fight. Yet she had to instruct her creation. How to do that quickly and efficiently?

She came to a decision. *Celine, we must go from here. You must test your new power while we have time.*

Where do we go, Mother?

You go to confront the minions of the Light and Dark before they are united with the rest of their kind. You need to measure yourself and take the measure of our enemies. Celine stood still, looking at the carved chairs and table, running her hand along the tabletop, made smooth by generations of hands and forearms resting on the worked stone. She could almost feel those men of the past, as she could feel the strength still residing in the carved rock. And there, of course, was the lesson: men come and go, as do their creations, but nature perseveres—or had, until now, until the Travelers interfered. Running her hands over the ancient stone, desecrated by the hammers and visions of man, she understood the danger earth faced. Celine turned and walked to Mother. Her eyes were dark brown and steady. A controlled mix of excitement and fury was building in her. Celine looked deep into Mother's eyes, and Mother felt the power of her creation. *Let us begin, Gaiea. I am ready* . At this point, Mother knew without a doubt that her creation—Celine, her daughter—was ready to duel the angeals of Light and Dark.

CHAPTER 25:

REVOLT

Kon-r dropped to one knee, blinded by the light of Cean's confirmation. A few moments passed before he could focus on the new Warrior. He smiled, remembering his own confirmation. The boy looked the part, and he, like all who came before, had been changed by his ordeal. The change was in his eyes, and, like the others, Cean emitted a certain force that he didn't have before—a strength, a presence, something that no one could miss or ignore. Kon-r could plainly see that Cean was, without a doubt, one of them. Kon-r looked to the Cath Angeal. She was smiling through her tears. She nodded just slightly, as if to recognize the truth of Kon-r's words, as if to confirm the changing nature of everything. Kon-r felt a strong connection to her. The other Warriors had voted as they had lived, and they were wrong. Only Kon-r recognized the truth of change. Kon-r gauged the others' reactions. They knew Cean had been confirmed, but they couldn't understand why. He had done the wrong thing, made the wrong choice. He had broken the rules. He should be dead.

Kon-r thought, *If these men, as valiant as they are, represent the past, then I am the present, and Cean is our future.* He looked to the Cath Angeal for confirmation. Reading his thoughts, she nodded. None of the others would have caught the movement. Kon-r felt no joy in this private communication. In fact, a deep sadness filled his soul. Never had the Warriors been divided over such an important decision. Kon-r experienced a deep foreboding; his blood ran cold. In his heart, he knew they would be marching to their last battle, and he would lead them to their deaths.

Considering this, his eyes never left those of the Angeal. Neither looked away, but there was no confirming nod this time—just a steady, penetrating stare, mutely asking the questions. *Are you ready, Kon-r? Can you do what is necessary one more time?*

Even though he had no idea what lay before him, it didn't matter. He was hers to command. Always had been, and always would be. He bowed his head slightly, then lightly jumped from the table and resumed his place of honor. His face was unreadable, his soul heavy with the weight of his friends' lives.

Kon-r turned to Cean and was startled to realize that he had been staring at him. Power seemed to crackle between them. Kon-r sensed Cean's dismay at his confirmation, but there was also a considerable amount of anger. Cean would not have forgotten the test of the Angeal. Grabbing the pommel of his sword with both hands, Cean raised it high above his head and slammed it, edge first, into the ancient stone. Sparks flew and a mighty *clang* reverberated around the chamber. The Table of Champions cracked into two great pieces and crashed to the tessellated floor.

The Warriors gasped. They jumped back from their ruined seat of power. Confusion reigned. Swords clattered on the hard floor, and the Warriors scrambled to retrieve their weapons. Cean, too, stepped away and raised his sword, waiting for the inevitable attack. He wanted none of this, whatever it was. Armed, the Warriors gathered to form a wedge with the First at the apex, ready to launch an assault. Kon-r, who stood away from the battle formation, had taken his weapon from the table as soon as he had seen Cean raise his sword. In fact, he grabbed his weapon as soon as he looked into Cean's eyes and recognized his rage. Kon-r didn't know what he would do if the First attacked. Would he stand aside and watch the inevitable slaughter, or would he fight at the new Warrior's side? Time seemed to stand still. No one moved. Cean presented a challenge they were ill-prepared to deal with.

The First was an implacable Warrior. With a violent scream he launched himself at Cean, blade held high, to deliver the killing stroke. Action froze. The First was suspended in air, his passionate leap now timeless, never to be completed. Cean stood still, coiled like a snake, ready to deliver a killing blow. The rest of the Warriors were locked a half step behind the First. The Chamber was silent. Kon-r saw the scene as if it was a painting. He sheathed his sword, turning at the same time to face the Cath Angeal. Controlling his anger, and in a voice quivering with emotion, he asked, "What is the purpose here, my lady? Why have you allowed this travesty? Have we not served you without fail? Have not these men given their lives in your service? This young man isn't responsible for what has happened: you are. What did you do to him to cause that reaction? What are you trying to accomplish by destroying thousands of years of honorable service?"

The Angeal met his gaze. Change was always difficult, particularly with men who prided themselves on being steadfast. She watched Kon-r's face, then Cean's: the present, Kon-r, and the future, Cean. Shattering the sacred center of the Warrior tradition in the Hall of Heroes? The Angeal was amazed by the brazen audacity of human activity. She had not planned for this to happen. She had not been sure, could not see, how the transition would happen. Cean's actions were his own. Free will in action, and yet it had served her purpose—the immediate, violent education of Kon-r Sighur and the other Warriors, because time was short, and the lesson had to be driven home. *Yes, Kon-r, it was you I had to shock into recognizing one central, inescapable fact: one age, his age, the Age of the Four, was soon to end, and another, whatever it would become, was soon to begin, and you, Kon-r Sighur, are responsible for making it happen.*

Before he could speak, she said, "Kon-r, listen and think. Tell me the future. Be honest with yourself, and ignore the heat of your emotions." Kon-r blinked. Hearing her words, thousands of bits of information began to align in his brain. Memories became immensely important. Insignificant actions—a death here, a lack of manners there, an argument over captured slaves that became a bitter subject within the officers' quarters, but most importantly, the flight of good men away from the Marfach Gardei—true men who could no longer see the value of the Gardei's mission and could not accept the endless death that accompanied Gardei campaigns. He thought of Torven Lok, best of the best, and realized that when men like Lok walked away, there was something deeply wrong.

The Angeal watched Kon-r's face carefully. She could see the emotion; she could read the thoughts in his head. "Would you continue, Kon-r? Knowing what you do, will you continue as my Warrior?"

"Do I have a choice, my lady? Is there work for me to do? And what will happen to my brothers, the Warriors of the past?"

This was just like Kon-r, just like the First, concerned more for others than for himself, she thought, once again amazed by the deep feelings these men aroused in her, not only on this battleground, but on all the other planets where the same fight had raged. They were the best, and they were alike wherever and whenever she found them. And they died for her. "They will defend Athlan one more time, Kon-r, before they meet their end. Their lives will not be wasted, although I can't foresee their end or yours. That power is denied me."

Kon-r tried to memorize every detail of the room, for he knew he would not see it again. He asked a simple question. "What would you have me do, my lady?" She was stunned by his honesty but had expected no less.

"Kon-r, I will show you what you will be up against. Deadly forces are on the move across the island. You are greatly overmatched. After you understand your peril, I want you to teach Cean everything you can in the short time left to you. While the future is unclear, he has been marked as Warrior, and it is unfair to send him into this battle ignorant of what has come before, or of what might yet become. At the same time, you will organize and lead the Marfach Gardei into their greatest battle."

"And their last, Angeal?" he asked.

"It might be, Kon-r. There is hope if one man stands to fight, but I can make no promises. Change is upon us, and nothing is guaranteed."

"Then show me this threat, but if Cean is to be my successor, should he not look upon the enemy as well?"

She nodded and made a small movement with her right hand. Cean, who was released from her power, moved like a man possessed and attacked. However, the First was not his target. Cean launched himself at the Angeal, and his sword whistled through the air, thirsty for her blood. The Cath Angeal did not flinch. A blurred shape passed between her and the newest Warrior, and a loud *clang* echoed through the Hall, as Kon-r's blade blocked Cean's. The two Warriors stood face to face, straining with all their might, swords locked at cross-guards, each incapable of backing off. Never had such a deadly, silent struggle taken place. Never had one Warrior faced off against another.

The Angeal spoke one word of command: "NO!" Both weapons flew from their hands. Within the space of one heartbeat, hand-to-hand combat began at a speed and level of violence never seen. Punches and kicks thudded and crunched onto flesh and bone. Grunts of pain punctuated rhythmic breathing from both Warriors. Once again, the Angeal had to use her voice. "Cease!" The men were thrust away from each other, unable to continue the fight. They stood, relaxed but deadly, mirror images. Their breathing slowed.

Cean sidestepped and grabbed his sword. In one smooth motion, he threw it at the Cath Angeal's heart. The point hit the invisible barrier, and waves of color radiated away in all directions, but the sword fell and clattered onto the stone surface. Cean stood still—frustrated, angry, and completely at sea. He studied the other Warriors in the chamber. They had not moved. He looked at Kon-r Sighur, deep into his eyes, and was surprised to see not hate, but compassion. Shifting his gaze to the Angeal, he said, "I have tried to kill you twice. I will try again if I can. Do with me what you will, but I will not play your game. I will not submit to your will. You will not control my actions. I am a free man. What do I have to do to prove it to you? Let these other men go. They, at least, are honest and honorable. I would rather fight and be killed by them than live to serve you."

The Cath Angeal remained silent. Kon-r, who had retrieved his blade, sheathed it and said, "Cean, I know what she put you through.

Each of us who wears these symbols has suffered exactly as you have suffered. Still, we stand and serve. Those behind you have overcome death to confirm you. We are all in this together, and I ask you to trust me and the valiant men of the past, if you cannot accept her. You know who and what I am. The power and honesty of the Warrior still courses through my veins. Put away your loss and listen."

Cean felt defeated. His anger vanished like smoke on the wind. He remembered all he had gone through climbing the streets of the citadel. He recalled the men he had fought—the men he had come to respect—and here was their leader, the best of them all, asking Cean to listen, as if they were equals. He had no choice. "Yes, Sighur, I will listen to you because, more than anyone, I know who and what you are. I have no quarrel with you. Speak. I will listen."

CHAPTER 26:

HEROIC FOOLS

Kon-r said, "My lady, release these men, and show us our peril. We need to know how to proceed. I can teach Cean, but only you have knowledge of the wider world and heavens above." Once again, the Angeal raised her hand and all in the hall were freed from their bonds. Shock registered on the faces of the Warriors who, the last they remembered, were attacking the newest Warrior candidate who had been found unacceptable. But he wasn't standing where he had been, and the First finished his leap and his massive death-cut, only to find no one there. His stroke sliced through empty air. Kon-r and Cean grinned at the ridiculous scene, but became serious as the First gathered himself and began to advance toward Cean with death in his eyes. Kon-r stepped between them and said, "Stop, good Ro. Things are not what they seem. The Angeal will explain all. Patience, men. Listen." The First stopped, and those behind him pulled up in a line across the hall. They sheathed their swords and stood perfectly still.

Kon-r said to Cean, "Stand with me, Warrior." They stood before the line of Warriors, and all faced the Angeal, waiting to hear what their destinies would be.

The Cath Angeal was deeply moved. She would sacrifice the lives of these men, as she had done in so many other situations. They knew they would die in her service, and still, they stepped forward to answer the call. "Other than Cean Mak-Scaire, the newest addition to your brotherhood—and, yes, he is one of you—each of you knows that I serve a higher purpose, and my power, such as it is, comes directly from that power. Throughout your lives, you have fought to protect certain principles. Each of you has faced dangerous foes that would destroy all that you have built, all that we consider good. No matter how hard you have fought, evil has not disappeared from earth. Kon-r can tell you: evil is on the rise, and the strength of Athlan has been fading while you have slept the sleep of the valiant."

The First raised an eye at Kon-r, who nodded to answer the silent question. "Yes, Ro, the long battle continues, and Athlan is no longer what it once was. Three of the Four are gone and have not been replaced. I, alone, am left, and as you know, there are now two Warriors.

I can guess what that means, as can you, but let us put guesswork aside, and listen to the Angeal."

She wasted no time. "Please, step back against the wall." The Warriors moved against the curved wall. The Angeal waved her left hand and the shattered table crashed against the wall on her left, clearing the beautiful floor. Pointing, she said, "Watch." The mortar joints melted together, forming a glass mirror that reflected the star-filled ceiling above. As they watched, the liquid surface clouded with mist. Through the mist, the Warriors could see dim shapes and sparks of light. The images began to clear, and the men sensed that they were approaching the earth from a great height. Seconds passed, and they began to recognize the island of Athlan. Hills, rivers, valleys, and plains; here was their home from above. They continued to descend, and the sparks of light resolved into raging fires that burned cities. Flames flowed to the sea from cracked hillsides. The old Warriors were horrified by the destruction of their country.

The First, the most controlled of men, uttered a strangled cry of grief. "Kon-r, is this true?"

Before Kon-r could answer, the Angeal said, "Yes, Ro, what you see is true. There is no deception. Athlan tears herself apart, and there is nothing I, nor anyone else, can do. But this is not what I want you to see. Behold." The picture at their feet became clearer, and the Angeal's soldiers saw large groups of campfires spread across the island. Each veteran campaigner recognized the fires for what they were: military bivouacs. Large campfires, each surrounded by men, suggested twelve separate armies of thousands, positioned across the island, creating a loose net around the Ban Castlean. Calculating automatically, each concluded that these positions were four, maybe five, hard, uphill marches away from the citadel.

They saw other, smaller groups spread across the land fitting no discernible pattern. *Probably loose groups of regular citizens trying to find a way to survive,* they thought.

Kon-r asked the obvious question. "Who are they, Angeal?"

She answered, "They are the soldiers of darkness, Kon-r. While you and the Warriors before you fought Athlan's battles far from home, evil grew in the shadows of our pride. As you have done my bidding, evil has had an equally long line of champions working against us, and they have enjoyed great success."

No one was satisfied with her answer. "But who are all of those people? How could they put twenty, thirty thousand men in the field against us? We have but a small fraction of that number."

"Like all people in power, Kon-r, you believe in your own rightness, but you have great difficulty realizing one essential fact: there is a vast group of people who do not see the world as you do. You stand in their way. You represent the established order. They are the new face of chaos. This problem is magnified by the pain and suffering caused by Athlan's collapse. Kon-r, there are people out there who are starving, afraid for their lives and their children's lives. They are desperate for someone to lead them to safety. Anyone will do. They will believe any promise that gives them hope. The Being that drives them now is called the Bas Croi. He is evil beyond comprehension. He and his masters have fought you and those before you all over the world, although you did not see them. They work through others, leading from the shadows. Fear is the coin of their realm, and the Bas Croi spends lavishly. Fear divides men, sets them against each other. The Bas Croi and his acolytes have convinced their followers that you, the Marfach Gardei, and the Four, are responsible for the destruction of Athlan. Croi tells them you are gathering a fleet to take you from the island. He tells them you have hoarded food behind the walls of the Ban Castlean. They want to believe. They need someone to rail against, someone to punish. Croi has promised them your ships, food, and wealth. By killing you, they have a chance to live. Do not underestimate the power of hate, for hate is the heartbeat of evil, and that bloody heart beats stronger. They prepare the final blow."

The First spoke for the group, "You said 'the final blow.' What did you mean, Angeal?" This was the difficult question. It always was, and, she supposed, always would be.

"There will be a battle soon. You know that. Whether it comes in five days or fifty-five does not matter. No allies will come to us. Athlan will not heal itself. We will fight. The Bas Croi has twelve captains, just as there are now twelve risen Warriors. The Bas Croi has dark power and wields it in the name of one who is not of this earth, as I am not of this earth. He goes by many names, but the Bas Croi knows him as the Anamarbaiche—Soul-Killer."

"And you?" asked the First. "What do you call him?"

"I know him as the Angeal Dorchada—the Angeal of Darkness. He and I fight on a different plane, and we have fought many times. We are evenly matched, it seems, but we continue to struggle, each hoping the next time will prove decisive. Your battle, though, is much different. If the Bas Croi is victorious, if the Warriors are wiped from the face of the earth, evil will claim a great victory, and darkness will spread throughout the land. Make no mistake: your deaths are what he seeks. Each one of you must die. If that happens, earth becomes isolated from the Light and will remain a dark planet until the end of time."

Mak-Scaire stepped forward and asked, "If we all die, and it appears that we will, and Athlan is destroyed and the world lost, what happens to you?"

She answered as sharply as he questioned. "I may win, lose, or draw my battle, Cean. So far, we have survived each contest. We suffer, but we continue to exist. If the test ends without a decision between him and I, and you all die, I will move on to another earth and prepare the way for the next Warrior, and the inevitable battle that will, in time, follow, or I will stay here and prepare for the next confrontation. Understand: I do not have freedom of choice in the matter. I was set on this path so long ago that none of you can grasp the meaning of so much time. I have fought in battles uncounted, always striving for victory against my foe. Planets I have saved for the Light are many, but always I am denied the final prize: the destruction of the Angeal Dorchada."

"A sad tale, but don't expect sympathy from me," said Mak-Scaire. "You throw away our lives while you count planets as if they were markers in a game. No matter what happens after the game, you move onto the next one, while the pieces lay strewn across the board, destroyed, or left to their own devices. Should I be happy with this? Should I be honored to be a board piece soon to be forgotten?" Cean implored the others for answers. "Tell me, anyone, is this what it really means to be a Warrior? Is this the cause you have fought and died for? Kon-r, we are tools and fools in this game. Tell me there is more she does not reveal."

"Yes, Cean, we are fools, for even if she did not exist, still we would have to fight evil in the world. We would still die. People would still suffer. Did not your mother and father die for reasons other than those of the Cath Angeal? Does she cause the destruction of Athlan? No. Cean, use your head. Do the marks on your arms tell you nothing of the nature of things? Power is beyond us. Look at her. See what she has done in this very chamber. Yes, we die fighting for a better idea, a better life than what the Bas Croi and his kind will try to force upon us. And yes, she moves on because her battle is never-ending, while ours is short. And yes, there is more, there must be more, or we, you, I, these men, wouldn't be here, wouldn't be like we are, but we will never know as she knows: we are simply men, men with extraordinary gifts, but men, nonetheless. Good men either fight for themselves and their people, or they fight for her. Until this moment, we fought for both and never questioned ourselves, our fate, or hers. You are the first to question, even after all you have seen. Perhaps you reflect our changing times and accept nothing on faith, for nothing is certain now, and maybe that is the lesson. Either way, we cannot remain idle; we must fight the Bas Croi. After all, we have nowhere to run." Kon-r smiled, and the Warriors of the past laughed and nodded in agreement: the final jest, soldiers' humor, laughing in the face of death. How can it be good? But it was.

"I find nothing funny in your words, Sighur," said the reluctant Warrior.

"No, you would not, Cean, for you are not one of us yet. We have a bond of shared experience, of effort, blood, and death in service of our country, in service of the great idea. You do not; you still see things from one point of view—selfish and inexperienced. You still have no understanding of what you are, or what is expected of you."

Cean interrupted. "Expected? Expected by whom? I didn't ask for any of this."

So strange, thought Kon-r, *this reluctant boy should come along at this crucial moment, or perhaps not so strange.* He said out loud, "Cean, you see things as a child sees them. Those who can must help. Those who can must lead. In an entire city of people, there are only a few who have the foresight and ability to get things done for the good of the many. Those who can must. Often, it is a thankless job because people in general are contrary, and while they clamor for what they think are their rights, they do not have the ability to lead others, nor will they make the sacrifices necessary to lead. Those marks on your arms, Cean. You have been given the ability to lead, to defend, to help. That is what we are on this earth to do. Will you think only of yourself, fisherman? Will you whine and bemoan your fate? Will you walk away because 'you didn't ask for any of this'? Do you think any of us has?"

All eyes were on Mak-Scaire. The Angeal watched his face closely. She needed this young man. If the coming battle proved inconclusive, as so many had, the Warrior tradition had to continue. Before anyone else spoke again, she said, "You have been selected as a Warrior. The marks on your arms prove it, and you have been confirmed before this group. You have a right to be here, maybe an obligation, but I will not hold you to it. You may leave if you wish. Walk back down the tunnel you came in. Once outside, no one will bother you. Leave the city, and do as you wish." No one had expected these words from the Cath Angeal. What was she doing? If Mak-Scaire refused to serve, he should be killed. He deserved no less.

Cean was as surprised as the rest. There it was. He could leave, just walk away, but to where, and to what end? Who was waiting for him? The answers slammed him—nowhere, nothing, no one. More to the point, what would he say to the men he had fought getting here? How about the man who had died for these same principles? What would he say to him? "Sorry, your life was worthless?" He knew better, and for the first time, he understood that even if he didn't believe anything she said, he could believe in the brotherhood. He would find no better, and if he was going to die, fighting alongside them would be a good ending.

Cean dropped to one knee and bowed his head. "I will stay, if these men will have me. Do you understand? These *men*, not you."

The Angeal stood before Cean, bent to grip his shoulders, and lifted him to his feet. *So be it.*

Holding his gaze, she said, "Will you help those who cannot help themselves?"

"Yes."

"Will you resist evil in all forms?"

Louder, he affirmed, "Yes."

"Will you stand and fight when no one else will share the burden?"

Louder still, he said, "Yes."

"Finally, swear to me that you will never give in to the Angeal Dorchada, the Bas Croi, or any of their minions, now and forever."

Softly, passionately, he said, "I do so swear, my lady." Tears ran down the faces of each Curadh, the hardest of men, as they remembered their own oaths, lives, victories, defeats, and deaths. Cean marveled at his own submission, but it felt good to belong, and he knew he had much to prove, if he was to hold his own in this company. The Warriors closed around Cean and put their hands on him; no words were spoken; acceptance and love shone from their eyes. He was home. He would fight.

THE END

about the author

C.T. Fitzgerald was born in South Buffalo, New York. While attending Canisius High School, Canisius College (B.A.), and Canisius Graduate School (M.A.), he also worked as a union, card-carrying, longshoreman (Local 1286) in the grain elevators of Buffalo, in the blast furnaces of Bethlehem Steel, as a bartender where his father and grandfather tended bar before him, and as a licensed teacher for the City of Buffalo.

Dr. Fitzgerald, (Kent State, Ph.D., Literature 2004), has been married to Kathleen for 45 years, and they are the parents of Ryan, Craig, and Tim and the happy grandparents, Pops and Nana, of Lachlyn, Shea, Emilia, and Connor.

He is weak in religious faith, but strong in the hope that we go to a far better place when the ballgame is over. Being a philosophical Cretan, Dr. Fitz's religious beliefs have been simply stated in the past: "Do unto others as you would have them do unto you." If humanity actually followed this easily understood rule, the world would be a much better place.

THE ADVENTURE

CONTINUES

IN

POWERS
REVEALED

The Threat of Angeals

Book 2

POWERS REVEALED

The Threat of Angeals Book 2

C. T. Fitzgerald

Made in the USA
Columbia, SC
01 August 2022

64320289R00124